"He was stalking her and planning his move."

Holly raised a hand to her forehead and gazed around the carnival. "They could be anywhere. What do we do?"

Ryan wasn't in uniform, so he didn't have his radio. He grabbed his phone. "I'll call it in. Get carnival security to do some looking."

Holly grabbed his hand. "No. No police. He said no police."

"I'll tell them to keep it low-key. He'll never know."

"He said no police or he will kill me. What kind of life would Georgia have then?" She looked up at him with those huge blue eyes that he'd been powerless against since he was twelve. "Please, Ryan."

He hated everything about this. The chances that Brody would be stopped and Georgia would be found without the help of police were slim and getting slimmer with every tick of the clock. He knew the statistics around parental kidnapping. He doubted there were really any statistics about parental abductions of famous children.

But he could never say no to Holly.

Jennifer Brown is the award-winning author of several middle grade and young adult novels, including her acclaimed debut, *Hate List*. Jennifer's Love Inspired novels include *Rescue at the Ridge*, *Peril at the Peak* and *Hunted at the Hideaway*, and she is also the nationally bestselling author of women's fiction novels under the pseudonym Jennifer Scott. She lives in Kansas City, Missouri. Visit her at jenniferbrownauthor.com.

Books by Jennifer Brown

Love Inspired Mountain Rescue

Rescue on the Ridge
Peril at the Peak
Hunted at the Hideaway

Visit the Author Profile page
at LoveInspired.com for more titles.

KIDNAPPED IN KANSAS

JENNIFER BROWN

LOVE INSPIRED
INSPIRATIONAL ROMANCE

LOVE INSPIRED®

INSPIRATIONAL ROMANCE

Recycling programs
for this product may
not exist in your area.

ISBN-13: 978-1-335-46841-3

Kidnapped in Kansas

For questions and comments about the quality of this book, please contact us
at CustomerService@Harlequin.com.

Love Inspired
22 Adelaide St. West, 41st Floor
Toronto, Ontario M5H 4E3, Canada
www.LoveInspired.com

Printed in U.S.A.

For what is a man advantaged,
if he gain the whole world, and lose himself,
or be cast away?
—*Luke* 9:25

For Scott

Acknowledgments

Thank you, first and foremost, to Cori Deyoe for her continued expertise, encouragement and friendship. I don't know where I would be without you there to help bounce ideas around, get to the bottom of plot problems or any of the other millions of things you do to support me.

Thank you to my editor, Johanna Raisanen, and thank you to everyone who worked on copyediting and design for helping Ryan and Holly get to their prettiest, best possible happily-ever-after. What a great team!

Finally, thank you to my family for understanding the importance of a Story That Must Be Heard, and for the unending gifts of ideas, inspiration, reassurance, coffee and quiet time so I can get the words on the paper. When it comes to you guys, I got exactly what I prayed for. I love you all the most!

PROLOGUE

If Holly had seen the strange woman waiting for them outside her apartment, she promptly would have taken Georgia's hand, turned, and walked the other way. But the woman was half-hidden, crouched in the bushes, and she didn't pop into the open until they'd already climbed the porch steps.

"Icefall," the woman breathed, emerging from the leaves. She had a *People* magazine—cover facing out, featuring the *Precipitators'* cast striking their fiercest hands-on-hips poses—clutched to her chest as tightly as if she were holding a baby. She was wearing a full Icefall costume. A superfan. "Icefall. It's you."

"No. She's not… We don't want…" Holly was juggling Georgia's backpack, lunch bag and a still-wet painting of a lion that Georgia had made in her pre-K art class, while trying to locate her keys, which had fallen to the bottom of her purse. She didn't want to set down anything. She'd done that before and the superfan had simply picked up Georgia's backpack and scurried away, leaving Holly to buy all new school supplies when she had barely been able to afford them the first time. "If you could just step back, ma'am..."

"Do you write your name yet, honey? Icefall? I-C-E-F—Oh, I can't believe I'm looking at real-life Icefall. Do you—does she do autographs? Maybe a picture? Can I get a picture? Give me the Icefall pose, sweetie." She pulled out her phone and snapped a photo of Georgia before Holly could move her child out of the way.

"No. No pictures, please." Holly tried nudging Georgia between herself and the door.

Georgia stared at the woman with her wide, blue eyes that looked tired from having resisted her nap that day, her arms slack at her sides. She didn't reach for Holly or cringe against Holly's leg, and that probably scared Holly most of all. The paparazzi were bad enough, but at least they were just doing their job. Superfans were, at times, way worse. Georgia was already so accustomed to her privacy being invaded that she just let it happen. What unhinged, fan-madness would she silently endure as a teenager, a young woman, an adult? Holly hated to think of it.

"Can I have a signature, though? It doesn't have to be perfect. Look, I brought a pen. Purple! Your favorite color! You can sign the cover right here where your face is." The woman wiggled a pen in the air.

"She doesn't do that." Holly finally got her hand around her keys. She pulled them out of her purse, stuck the key in the door and turned just in time to see the fan do the unthinkable: reach for her child.

"Look at that hair, though. It's real. I always wondered if it was real or if Hollywood put a white wig on her. I can't believe it's real. I bet a lock of that hair would bring a pretty penny. Not that I would ever sell it, of course. But if I were to get my hands on one, it'd sure be priceless."

"Don't touch her! Stay away!" Holly's yell startled both the woman and Georgia. Georgia's lip trembled, but in true Georgia form, she still didn't cry. Holly reached down and grabbed her daughter's hand. "Come on, Gee."

The lion painting fluttered to the ground as Holly pulled Georgia inside the building, turning to make sure the door latched behind her. What had that woman meant about getting her hands on a lock of her daughter's hair? Would she have taken one if Holly hadn't gotten Georgia out of there? How? Did she have scissors or would she have just yanked? Either scenario made Holly feel cold. This was a new level of fandom that they hadn't yet endured.

Georgia whimpered and pointed at the lost lion painting but still didn't protest as Holly whisked her upstairs.

"Sorry, baby, I'll come back down and get it as soon as that creepy woman is gone." But Holly knew it wouldn't be there. The woman, unable to secure an autograph or a lock of hair, would settle for the painting, which would never hang on the refrigerator like an ordinary child's painting would. Holly was certain she would later see it on an online auction site. And the woman was right—it would bring a pretty penny.

Once inside her own apartment with the door locked behind her, Holly rested her back against it for a long minute, her heart beating out of her chest. Not for the first time, she wished she'd never entered Georgia in that cute toddler competition two years ago, or said yes to the ice cream commercial after that. And, especially, she wished she'd never signed Georgia on to play the part of "Icefall" in the *Precipitators* superhero movie that swept the nation over the holidays. Life had been a whirlwind ever since and not in a good way.

She took a few moments to slow her breathing, allowing Georgia to trot off to her bedroom to reunite with her favorite stuffed kitty cat after a long day in pre-K, and then picked up her phone.

She called the police first. And then Jim, her manager at the grocery store, who was none too pleased that she was asking to use all her accumulated vacation time, effective immediately.

And then she called her mom in Garnett, Kansas, to say the six words she'd been obsessing over since Georgia's newest contract offer had come in.

"Mom, I need to come home."

ONE

Garnett, Kansas, hadn't changed a bit, and Holly Shipley was glad of it. Small, flat, friendly and a little sleepy. Greens and golds and fields and farms and cows serenely grazing on rolling hills. A far cry from bustling, expensive San Fernando Valley where she'd been scraping by. A total change of pace was just what the doctor ordered.

Like her car, Holly was drifting into town on fumes—burnt out from the stress of bills she could barely cover with her paycheck from the grocery store and the huge decision whether to sign an agreement that could both make things far better and far worse for Georgia and her. Most people prayed for fame and fortune. Georgia had the fame, and the "fortune" was tucked away in a savings account, but Holly wasn't sure either of those things were what they were cracked up to be. The fortune was small. And the fame was scary. In a world riddled with fickle and sought-after celebrity status, Holly had somehow stumbled in and couldn't find her way out.

Be careful what you pray for. You never know when

your prayers will be answered. And you never know when they'll stop being answered, too.

And, boy, wasn't that the truth? God sure seemed to have selective hearing when it came to Holly's prayers. At least, that was what she thought when she was feeling particularly bitter about her predicament.

The problem with calling it quits on Georgia's budding movie career? There was now money set aside for the little girl's future, which was all Holly ever wanted for her daughter and had feared she would never be able to provide. Holly hadn't touched a dime of Georgia's Icefall earnings. She was still buying cheap hot dogs on an employee discount to get by and hand-sewing the dresses they wore to the premieres.

She didn't want her daughter to stress and scrabble the way she'd had to, but she hadn't counted on having to evade boundary-less fans, push her child beyond her limits of exhaustion because someone needed an interview, field continual requests for impromptu reenactments of that famous volcano scene or suffer repeated sudden blindness from a surprise paparazzi shot when the poor kid was just trying to play. She'd started to wonder if being famous was worse stress than being tight on funds.

She needed to go home to Garnett. To just get away. To think.

"Hey, Gee, we're here," she said, reaching into the back seat and rubbing Georgia's little leg, which dangled down from her booster seat. It was clammy. Garnett in July was hot, and the air conditioning in Holly's car left a lot to be desired. She popped open her door for a fresh breeze, and the rising and falling buzz of the cicadas filled the car. Instant nostalgia. Let there be no doubt—she was back in Kansas. No paparazzi here. No creeps in the bushes trying to get a lock of hair. Just Holly, her daughter, her mother, and a lot of quiet time to figure out how to ask God for help without making things worse.

The little girl stirred, then opened her eyes, squinting against the sun. Her face puckered up as if she were about to whine. But one of the many things that made Georgia Shipley such a perfect child star was her disposition. She was almost never cranky. She was definitely not a crier. She had a sunshiny personality that matched the gold flecks in that famous white-blond hair of hers.

"Come on," Holly said. "Nana Cheryl is waiting. Are you hungry? I'll bet she's got something good for us to eat."

Georgia perked up. "Like cookies?"

Holly nodded. "Maybe even brownies, too."

Sure enough, Holly's mom was standing at the front door, wearing a flour-sprinkled apron—*a good sign for the brownie situation, Holly thought*—and waving happily. Holly waved back, took a deep, cleansing breath and got out of the car. If perspective was around here anywhere, she was determined to find it.

An hour later, Holly and Georgia were unpacked, cleaned up, and enjoying grilled cheese sandwiches and bowls of homemade tomato soup in Nana Cheryl's cozy, red-and-white-checkered kitchen. In the middle of the table sat a platter heaped with fresh-baked brownies.

"I grew the tomatoes myself, you know," Cheryl said, nodding toward the sliding glass door, which looked out onto the backyard that was almost entirely taken up by a lush garden. Holly had grown up in that backyard and had seen swing sets and trampolines, clubhouses and one greedy strawberry patch come and go. She liked the current version of the backyard—the garden-and-critters style let her know that her mom was finally, after decades of toiling away as a single parent trying to make ends meet, relaxing and doing things for herself. "I've had so many this year I've been eating tomato everything for weeks. Tomato sandwiches, tomato salad, tomato soup."

"Tomato cupcakes," Georgia said. She giggled over her spoon, sending a dribble of soup back down into the bowl.

"Tomato…ice cream," Holly said, wiggling her eyebrows at Georgia.

"Tomato pants!" Georgia said.

"Plants?"

"No, Nana, *pants*!"

"Pants aren't food, silly," Holly said.

But Cheryl nudged her granddaughter. "And I've been wearing tomato hats and tomato gloves, too."

The little girl dissolved into giggles, and then she began singing the soup commercial she was supposed to shoot in two weeks. "S-U-P, soup for me. Try pe-ger-greeem. It's yummy."

"S-*O*-U-P," Holly corrected. "And it's Pedigreen."

"Sounds like a dog food," Cheryl noted.

"A dog food that no dog wants to eat," Holly agreed. *And a commercial directed by a cranky snoot that nobody wants to work for. If Georgia doesn't correct that misspelling and mispronunciation, she just might find out how cranky he can get.*

"Pe-ge-greem soup, it's yummy!" Georgia held up her spoon triumphantly. "But it's not for dogs, Nana. It's for people."

Holly's mom laughed, but Holly was distracted by movement in the backyard next door. She sat forward, her stomach fluttering. Surely she wasn't seeing who she thought she was seeing. "Is that…?"

"Hmm?" Her mom followed her gaze. "Oh, Ryan Oldham? Yes, his parents moved to Florida. Sold him the house, from what I understand. He just moved in a few weeks ago. I'll miss Trish and Perry. They're good people. But so is Ryan. He's a police officer now, did you know?"

"Uh-huh," Holly said absently, still staring. She actually didn't know. She hadn't seen hide nor hair of Ryan Oldham in years. But, given the protective, tactical-minded person she remembered him to be, policing fit. "Is it just him living there?"

"Do you mean, is he married? No, I don't think he is. No wife, no kids. Just him."

Holly softly chewed her lip, letting herself be taken back years.

Ryan Oldham. The literal Boy Next Door. They'd met over the backyard fence in middle school, when Ryan or one of his friends—they never did admit who did it—threw a Frisbee over the fence and accidentally bonked new-to-the-neighborhood Holly Hampton in the middle of the forehead. Instant mortification for everyone. Ryan had been apologetic as Holly handed it back to him, absently rubbing the spot where it had made contact. They'd laughed at the moon-shaped mark it left on her skin, and an instant friendship was born.

They'd been like peas and carrots all through high school. The more Holly got to know Ryan, the more she wanted to be near him. By the time they were graduating from high school, she was full-on smitten. Holly never told Ryan that she had a huge crush on him, thinking there was no way someone like Ryan Oldham would feel that way about her—she was skinny and pale and shy, and he was muscular and tan and popular. In time, they both dated other people. And Holly met bad boy Brody Shipley and fell in love.

And ten days after high school graduation, she ran away to marry Brody, and Ryan let her go.

She had never spoken to Ryan again.

But she'd thought about him. Only a million or so times. And here he was. Right next door. Like neither of them had ever left.

She got up and drifted to the door, barely hearing Georgia and her mom, who'd gone back to bantering about tomatoes. Ryan had been a cute middle schooler and a dreamy teen. But he'd grown into a man who was effortlessly handsome. Light brown hair cut close on the sides and left a little longer on top, brushed back in waves lying obediently in place as if they were perfect just because he wanted them to be. Stubble running across his jaw, but not so much that you couldn't still see the slight indentation in his chin. Biceps that popped out from under his T-shirt as he pulled weeds near the fence line. He stopped to wipe sweat from his forehead, those biceps rippling, and saw Holly staring. His brow creased, then smoothed, and a smile spread across his face. He waved, and Holly lifted a shy hand in return. Peas and carrots.

"I'll be right back," she said. She pulled open the door and stepped outside, hardly noticing the oppressive wall of heat slamming into her.

She was focused on one thing and one thing only: a reunion that she'd daydreamed about more times than she could count.

Ryan couldn't believe what he was seeing. Holly Hampton, er, Holly *Shipley*, was walking across the backyard next door toward the fence. It was like being transported backward in time, all the way to middle school, a surreal feeling he'd had many times since buying his parents' house and moving back to Garnett.

Somehow, she was even more beautiful than he remembered her, and he would have never thought that possible. He didn't even feel himself drop the fistful of weeds he was holding or slowly rise to meet her. He was so captivated by the way she smoothly picked her way through the garden, as if her feet weren't even touching the dirt, and the way the late afternoon sun shone behind her, lighting up the gold in her light blond hair and shadowing her face so that the blue in her eyes flashed out at him, mini reflections of the cloudless sky. There was something trepidatious about her mannerisms—a nervous entwining of her hands, a hesitant rise in her shoulders—that endeared her to him even further. He'd forgotten that she was shy.

"Holly Shipley," he said. "As I live and breathe."

She stopped, curtsied, then laughed and closed the distance to the fence, her arms held out as if for an embrace. But at the last moment, she turned timid and gripped the fence instead. "Ryan Oldham, right where I left you." She pushed a lock of hair behind one delicate ear. "This is weird, right?"

"Definitely weird," he said. "Kind of like…full circle or something. I have an irresistible urge to run and fetch a Frisbee."

She rubbed her forehead. "You remembered. I was sort of hoping you would forget one of the more humiliating days of my preteen life."

"Never. How could I forget the beginning of a friendship for the ages?" They both laughed, and then there was a pause as their eyes locked. Ryan swore something like lightning passed between them.

Except friendships for the ages don't suddenly stop when someone runs away, he thought.

"How's Brody?" It popped out without Ryan thinking it through. Had he sounded defensive? Desperate? Sarcastic?

She shrugged. "I wouldn't know. I've haven't heard a peep from him in a couple of years." She held up her left hand and wiggled her fingers. "Divorced. Well, abandoned, really. And then divorced."

"Ah. I'm sorry to hear that," Ryan said, and then there was an awkward beat during which he supposed they were both wondering if that was true. *Was* he sorry to hear that it hadn't worked out with Brody? No. But if she were hurt by what had happened with Brody, he was definitely sorry.

"What about you? What are you up to these days?"

He shrugged. "Just rattling around this old house."

"It's not that old."

"Old enough to need repairs. I feel like my dad, out doing yardwork and thinking that the trim around the back door needs to be repainted."

Holly laughed, "Okay, well, now you do sound like your dad. He was always bustling around fixing things."

"Only now he's doing more beaching than bustling."

"Good for him," Holly said. "He earned it. But that door—it does need paint. Want help with it?"

Ryan stepped away from the fence, waving his hands as if to ward her off. "No way. If I remember correctly, you are the worst painter in the entire world. Do I need to remind you about the fence incident our freshman year?"

"Hey, I've gotten better. It's been a long time, Oldham. You don't know what kind of skills I've picked up. For all you know, I'm a professional painter now."

"Are you?"

"No."

"I didn't think so. I would have been very surprised." They laughed with the same ease they'd had as kids. "It has been a long time, though. In some ways, it feels like we never left. For a second there, I thought you were an illusion. That maybe I was stuck in eleventh grade, never to be released into adulthood."

"I totally get that same feeling." The back door she had just come out of slid open, and a little girl who was the spitting image of Holly stepped out. Ryan felt a sense of déjà vu. He'd seen the child somewhere before. Did she look that much like Holly? No, that wasn't quite it. She…

"Oh! Wow! Is that…?"

"Mommy, Nana's gonna let me pick more tomatoes," the little girl said, trotting over to Holly and wrapping an arm around her leg. She looked up at Ryan with the same blue eyes as Holly's, taking him back years.

He looked from the girl to Holly and back. "Mommy? I didn't know you had a daughter."

Holly nodded as she ran her hand through the little girl's hair. "This is Georgia. Georgia, say hi to Mommy's friend, Ryan. Or… I guess… Mr. Oldham." She wrinkled her nose and bit her bottom lip—a habit of hers he'd somehow forgotten, even though he had always found it endearing. "That sounds stuffy. *Mr. Oldham.* The only person I ever heard call you that was Coach Jeffries."

Ryan chuckled. He hadn't thought about Coach Jeffries in a while. "Surely Jeffries isn't around anymore." He bent to the little girl's eye level. "Hi, Georgia. Nice to meet you."

"Hi," Georgia said, not at all shy. She must have gotten that trait from Brody.

He felt a little silly with what he was about to say,

but he couldn't help himself. "Did you know that you look an awful lot like a girl in the movies?"

As if she'd been rehearsing for this moment, Georgia dropped back into a fighting stance, her hands held out in front of her, claw like, her teeth bared in a grimace. "Feel the freeze!" She flicked her arms up and down dramatically. "Now's when you're s'posed to die," she whispered. "If you don't know what to say, you're just s'posed to say 'line.'"

"Oh! Right." Ryan clutched his chest, let out a strangled cry and collapsed to the ground, giving his legs a couple of extra kicks, which elicited delighted laughter from the little girl. He waited, then jumped up again. "But what's this? He has…plant power!" He brandished one of the weeds he'd dropped earlier and then hurled it over the fence with great effort, as if it weighed a hundred pounds. It landed on Georgia's foot. Right on cue, she squealed, whirled in circles and fell to the ground.

"A…melting…plant…" She gasped, then went still with her tongue hanging out the side of her mouth.

Ryan held his arms up. "Victory! Roots Runner wins again!"

Holly laughed and applauded while Ryan took a bow. Cheryl called for Georgia, and Georgia scrambled to her feet and took off with a quick, over-the-shoulder *bye*.

"She's awesome," he said.

"Thank you." Holly beamed, looking after her daughter. "She is pretty amazing, if I do say so myself."

"So do you hear that a lot?" he asked. "That your daughter looks like the girl in the *Precipitators* movie?"

"I do," Holly said. "And that's because she is."

His eyes grew wide. "Your daughter is Icefall?"

Holly nodded, and he thought maybe he picked up on a tiny bit of...sadness? Regret? He couldn't be sure—he only knew that it was something not altogether pleasant. "And the toddler tearing up the house in those diaper commercials. And soon to be the Pedigreen Soup Girl. Although we're struggling a bit on the pronunciation of that one."

"Probably because it sounds like—"

"Dog food? Yes, I know."

"Wow," Ryan said. "She's a star."

"Yes," she said. "She is." She paused for a beat, then changed the subject. "Mom says you're a police officer."

"Garnett's finest," he said.

"You always tried to keep the peace," she said.

"Still do."

"So you like it? You're happy?"

His ex-girlfriend Morgan's face tried to push into his mind, unbidden, her smile bright as she accepted her academy diploma and paused for a photo. She was practically glowing, and as soon as the picture was taken, her eyes found him in the crowd. Somehow her smile grew brighter as his dimmed. Morgan was perfect in so many ways. But he knew in that moment she was in love with him and would be expecting more out of him than he could give. She wanted a future.

It had been a year since he'd broken it off with Morgan. It still smarted, no matter how hard he prayed for peace and acceptance. Seeing Holly again only made it worse.

"I am," he lied. "Very happy."

There was a weird, expectant pause as if Holly knew he'd been lying. The cicadas started their song again. Holly scratched the side of her neck as she turned to watch Georgia and her mother creep around in the garden plucking vegetables off the plants.

"Mom says the Anderson County Fair was this weekend," Holly said. "Tonight's the last night. You going?"

He hadn't really planned on it, but there was something about being in Holly's presence again that made him unable to resist even the vaguest invitation. The years had vanished like morning mist. Was this the answer to his prayers? God's way of letting him know that it was time to accept and move on? "Yeah. Sure."

She beamed. "Great! We can talk more there."

"Definitely."

Georgia called for her mommy, and Ryan made an excuse about needing to get back inside. Holly drifted away from the fence, looking back with that smile that used to light up his entire world—and still did. He hadn't been this excited about a fair since he was a kid.

Two hours later, all cleaned up and humming with anticipation, Ryan stepped outside his house to go meet Holly at the fair. He'd spent those entire two hours in conversation with God, trying to understand what exactly it meant for Holly to walk back into his life at exactly the time he was trying to let the past go. Maybe this was no coincidence that they'd both come home to Garnett at the same time. Maybe this was how things were supposed to go from the beginning.

Maybe, just maybe, this would be his chance to be with Holly. Seven years later than he'd hoped, but they could make up for lost time.

Just as he began to get into his car, an engine revved behind him. He turned to see a white sedan pulling away from the curb opposite Cheryl's house.

Inside was someone he would recognize a mile away.

The same someone who took Holly away in a different car seven years ago.

Brody Shipley.

The car sped up and took off, quickly rounding the corner and out of sight.

Ryan was flooded with disappointment.

Maybe he was misinterpreting whatever it was that God was trying to tell him. Maybe it was foolish for him to be this excited about seeing Holly again. It was rash to think that one conversation at the fence, followed by one invitation to the fair that everyone in Garnett attended, meant anything. Holly and Brody shared a child. If Brody came around, of course Holly would want to let him in. For all Ryan knew, Holly and Brody were rekindling what they once had, and if he were at all smart, he would shut down his heart and refuse to let Hurricane Holly back in.

After all, he had lost Holly to Brody Shipley once before.

He did not want to feel the pain of losing her again.

TWO

Like the rest of Garnett, the Anderson County Fair had changed little since the last time Holly had been there. Or maybe it was just the scent of warm powdered sugar sprinkled on funnel cakes straight out of the fryer that instantly took her back to her teen years, the excited yips from the midway, the dings of bells announcing that prizes had been won, the rumble and squeak of rides starting and stopping, the combination of which grabbed hold of her aching heart and soothed it with memories of good days gone by.

But she remembered the past in a different way: the sour grief of not ever knowing her father, the loneliness of having a mom who worked three jobs to keep them afloat, the chores and the fights and the things that eventually led her to Brody, whose tattoos and freedom from the constraints of school were so alluring they were intoxicating. She didn't so much choose Brody as she was chosen by him, which made it all the more painful a few years later to watch for a car that never came home, leaving her with a three-year-old who adored her daddy and a bunch of empty prayers that he would come back for that three-year-old.

Who had time for fairs when there were broken hearts to repair?

Georgia had never been to a small-town fair. She'd been to Disneyland and Legoland and Six Flags and the places where child stars go when the people in their lives decide to let them be children for a few hours. But she'd never eaten an onion blossom in a Styrofoam bowl or made sand art in a glass bottle or zipped down a slide on a burlap sack. Georgia almost seemed nervous, insisting on bringing her favorite stuffed cat for comfort, and Holly, knowing full well that Kitty would need a thorough wash after Georgia had gone to sleep that night, had relented. Yes, Kitty could ride some rides, too.

Georgia buzzed and flitted around the fairgrounds like an overeager moth, lighting in one place for only moments before moving on to the next. She made a friend at the fishbowl ring toss—a little girl with dark ringlets and dirty knees, whose parents were busy running a handmade jewelry booth in the craft tent and happy that another adult was keeping an eye on their child for a few moments—and went into overdrive. Holly felt like she was walking in circles, delighted to see such joy in Georgia, but also exhausted from months of sleeplessness and days of cross-country travel.

Not to mention, with all this movement, it was almost impossible to look for Ryan in the crowd. To be perfectly honest, she had been drawn to the fair by the idea of getting to experience it with him. After twenty-three hours in the car she would have been happy as a clam to sit on the couch with a book and a lemonade for a few hours.

"Why don't we go to the hay maze?" Holly suggested. She was grateful when the girls agreed. There were picnic benches just outside the hay maze and a food truck selling apple nachos and root beer nearby.

The girls plunged into the maze, filled with squeals and laughter, and Holly took her food to a table and sank down gratefully. She ate and people-watched, keeping an eye out for the one person she hoped to see most. She checked her watch. She'd expected him to be here by now. Maybe he'd decided not to come, after all—a thought that thoroughly disappointed her.

But just as she had convinced herself to give up on the idea that she was going to reconnect with Ryan, he wandered into the midway, calmly alert to everything happening around him.

"Ryan!" she called, waving.

He glanced around, searching for the source of his name, and then his eyes found her. She thought she saw a mix of emotions cross over his face and wasn't sure if all of them were positive.

"You made it," she said, scooting over to make room for him on the bench. To her surprise, he lowered himself to the bench on the other side of the table instead.

"Wouldn't miss it." He offered a smile that didn't really convince her, his eyes searching everywhere but her direction.

"How long has it been since you've gone to the fabulous Anderson County Fair?" she asked.

"Many years."

"And?"

"Pretty much exactly as I remembered it."

"Same. I even think that's still the family who always made the kettle corn when we were kids. Do these kinds of things exhaust you? As an officer, I mean? Are you always looking for something to happen?" Holly realized she was rambling, nervous.

He shrugged. "I'm not on duty. But, generally, no. I've always been aware. That's why I took this job. It was a good fit. I would have been keeping an eye on the crowd regardless."

Why did she feel like she was conducting a job interview? This was not the Ryan who'd been standing across the fence from her. That Ryan had been open and flirty. Something had happened. Something to make him pull away. The man who'd been only hours before pretending to be frozen to death by Icefall was now a little frosty himself. It threw her. Or maybe she'd misjudged the chemistry she'd felt, had seen a reunion she'd wanted to see, rather than one that had actually happened. She squirmed, her mind racing for things to say. She pointed at the Whirly Swirly ride.

"Do you remember when we rode that thing like twenty times, and…?"

He chuckled, the old Ryan peeking through again. "Don't remind me. I still get queasy just looking at it. We drank all that red cream soda before getting on."

"And cotton candy. Don't forget the cotton candy that we ate."

"I am trying to forget that, though," he said. "I'm sure the guy who was running the ride that day is still trying to forget it, too."

They laughed, and it felt good—really good. These were the sweet moments that Holly missed. In some ways, they were the last purely good memories she had. Only six months into being Mrs. Brody Shipley, sweet moments died. Just dried up and blew away. She was left the shriveled, unsmiling wife to a humorless and dangerous man. And she missed Ryan deeply. The friend who could have been more, if only he'd asked.

"Apple nacho?" She slid the paper bowl across the table.

"Hey, Georgia's mom?"

Holly looked down to see the little girl who'd been playing with Georgia standing near her knee. Holly leaned forward. The girl was cute. She wondered if Georgia would be just like this if she hadn't been busy in Hollywood. Sometimes Georgia seemed delightfully precocious; other times, she had the world-weariness of a jaded forty-year-old. "What do you need, honey?"

"Georgia's not playing nice," the girl said.

Holly frowned. "Oh, no. That's not okay. What's she doing?"

"She won't come out."

Holly's frown turned into confusion. "Won't come out of what?"

"She won't come out of her hiding spot. We're playing hide-and-seek. She hides real good. But she won't come out. And I'm tired of being *It*. I want to play something else."

"Okay," Holly said. "I'll tell her to come out and play fair. Hold down the bench for me?" She said the last to Ryan, who'd picked up an apple slice and bitten into it.

"Sure thing."

"Come on, sweetie. Let's go tag Georgia and make her *It*."

The girl popped a thumb into her mouth and took Holly's hand with her free hand.

The maze, created by stacks and stacks of baled hay, felt much bigger on the inside than it looked on the outside. Holly was surprised by how many children were romping around in there, jumping from hay bale to hay bale, pouncing from above into mounds of loose hay. She was even more surprised by how many grown adults were wandering around inside with their kids, playing like overgrown children themselves. So many crevices, so many dead ends for Georgia to hide in. Charming, but a little overwhelming.

At first, it was fun. Holly let go of the little girl's hand and skulked around corners, jumping at the last minute, ready to pronounce, *Got you!* But, soon, fun gave way to concern. Then concern to worry, as she'd leapt into every possible corner and still no Georgia. A part of her was irritated that Georgia was hiding this well and for this long. It was rude at best. Another, deep-down part of her knew that Georgia would never hide this well. Something was wrong.

"Georgia!" she called. "It's time to come out now." She paused to listen for a response but only heard the squeals and shouts of dozens of kids, none of which were her daughter. "Georgia? Come out. You're not being a fun playmate to your new friend."

She started walking again, trying to ignore the tingling feeling in her chest that she recognized as the same fear response she'd felt when that superfan on the stoop had reached for her daughter's hair.

"Georgia? Come out, now! I'm not kidding."

She spun in circles, scanning the kids on top of the bales, hoping that, in her growing fear, she was just somehow not hearing or seeing her child. But there was nothing. As she quickened her pace, bumping into people and scraping her arms against the hay while trying to squeeze past them, the tingling became stronger and sharper, and her head felt swimmy.

"Georgia! This isn't funny! The game is over. Come out!"

Holly was so lost in her own growing fear, she didn't realize that she had begun running—that people had stopped what they were doing to stare at her, parents exchanging worried glances, then gawking into nearby corners themselves, as if to help locate the child. She didn't realize that her voice had gone funny—panicked and rough and strangled. "Georgia!"

It occurred to her that it was entirely possible that Georgia had come out and had maybe gone to the table where she left Ryan. She was sure he would've kept Georgia there, knowing that Holly and the little girl were looking for her. She plunged out of the hay maze and went back to the picnic table.

Ryan was still there, still eating apple slices. But he was standing, a wary look on his face. "What's wrong?"

Holly swallowed, trying to calm herself. She didn't want to be *that* mom—the one who panicked at the first sign that something wasn't what she thought it should be. To cry *missing child* and then have said child show up at her hip moments later. She could only imagine how many cell phone cameras were pointed at her. How many people would post it online later. And once they put it together who the missing child was, the tabloids would have a heyday with it. *Icefall's mom loses it—and loses Icefall—in public.* Humiliating. When she finally got her hands on Georgia, they would have a long talk about wandering and hiding and scaring Mommy. "We can't find Georgia. She didn't come out here, did she?"

He shook his head, brushed his hands off and came out from behind the picnic table. The instant seriousness on his face worried Holly even more. He crouched to eye level with Georgia's little friend. Holly had forgotten that the child was with her.

"Do you have any idea where she might be hiding? Any idea at all?"

The little girl shook her head.

Ryan shifted to look up at Holly. "Would she have left the hay maze without telling you? Wandered off?"

"No. I mean... I don't think so. I don't know." Holly glanced at the maze, then turned back to him. "She's never been anywhere like this before. She wouldn't have done it at a place like Disneyland, but I can't say for sure... Maybe she felt safe enough here to wander?

That's not like her. She's very responsible for a five-year-old."

But a responsible five-year-old is still a five-year-old.

"I'll stay here and watch the hay maze for her if you want to look around elsewhere."

She nodded. "Okay, I…"

"I think maybe she went with that man," the little girl said, tugging on Holly's hand.

Holly and Ryan stared at the little girl.

"What? What man?" Holly asked.

"The one she was talking to," the little girl answered.

"What!" Holly could no longer hide her fear from herself. Could Georgia have been lured away by a predator? Another fan, or worse, someone who had no idea who she was and was just after her because she was a pretty little girl with striking blond hair? "What man was she talking to?"

She must have frightened the little girl, because the girl began to cry.

Ryan placed his hands on the little girl's shoulders to calm her. He looked her in the eyes and spoke with a steady, even tone. "Did you see Georgia talking to someone?"

The little girl nodded.

"What did he look like?"

The little girl shrugged, crying harder. "I don't know."

"He was a grown-up, though?"

The little girl nodded again. "I thought he was her daddy," she said through hiccups.

Holly and Ryan exchanged looks again, and Ryan stood. Holly shook her head. "Impossible."

"Did he say anything about coming to the festival today?" Ryan asked.

"Why would he say anything to me? We haven't heard from Brody in two years."

"Until today," Ryan said.

Holly shook her head again. "What do you mean?"

"He was at your house today, right?"

"No. He wasn't."

"I saw him. He was pulling away from the curb as I was leaving to come here."

Holly couldn't take in what she was hearing. Brody was at her house? But why? How did he even know she was in Garnett? Why was *he* in Garnett? Ryan had to be mistaken. It had been many years. Maybe seeing her made him see Brody in someone else, just by association.

Holly swiveled to face the little girl. "Why did you think the man was her daddy?" she asked, trying not to scare the child even more but unable to calm the storm that was happening inside her. "Did she call him that?"

"No, he just called her *my baby Georgie-bean*," the little girl said. "I thought it was a funny name."

This time, Ryan and Holly seemed to have a whole conversation without saying a word. They were both thinking the same thing—if Brody was around and Holly didn't know about it, and he had Georgia with him—they had a big, big problem.

They took off in opposite directions, each entering the hay maze at the far ends, Holly calling Georgia's name and Ryan ordering everyone out. They met somewhere in the middle, panting, and only paused for a second before turning and going back the way they'd come.

By the time they reconvened outside the maze, there was a crowd. And, yes, many cell phones were pointed at Holly. But she no longer cared about the press. Georgia was gone, and she had no idea why Brody—if it was Brody—had taken her. He hadn't shown any interest in her since walking away. So why now?

"I'll search that way. You search over there?" Ryan pointed again in opposite directions.

Holly nodded. But then her cell phone rang, and an unknown number popped up on her screen. She put her hand on Ryan's arm to stop him. "Wait."

She brought the phone to her ear, but before she could even say a word, Brody's voice ripped through her like a bad memory. Her body began quaking. It had been so long since she last heard his voice that she'd forgotten the fear that came with it.

"Holly, Holly, Holly. Talk about a blast from the past," he said. "Did you miss me? I didn't miss you."

"Do you have Georgia? Where is she?"

He continued as if she'd never said a word. "I discovered the little secret you were keeping from me, so I just had to say hello."

"What…?" Holly's voice had way too much breath in it. She gasped for air. "Keeping what secret from you, Brody? I'm not keeping any secrets. Is Georgia okay?"

"Oh, but you are. Well, you *were*. It's all out in the open now. No thanks to you."

"What are you talking about? Give the phone to Georgia."

"There I was, Holly, minding my own business, eating my popcorn, enjoying the new *Precipitators* movie, and I realized—hey, that kid playing Icefall looks awfully familiar. She looks just like Georgia. Surely she's not Georgia, though. Not *my* Georgia. Because if she was *my* Georgia, you would have let me know. I mean, it seems reasonable, doesn't it, that you would tell someone that his own child is a movie star? But guess what? I was wrong. A little internet search on my phone right there in the theater told me that Icefall indeed was my child, and her mother indeed kept me in the dark about it. Can you imagine how I must have felt? How betrayed I felt, finding out your secret that way?"

"I'm not keeping anything secret," she repeated, the terror inside her pushing her words out in a high-pitched squeak. "You left us."

"Just listen. For once in your life, stop talking and listen!"

Holly nodded even though she knew he couldn't see her.

"You thought you could turn our daughter into a celebrity and I would never find out, and that shows how clueless you really are. And I know you did it so you could get rich and cut me out, but you're wrong. I won't be cut out."

"I wasn't cutting you out. You left. You would have known exactly what *my* child was doing if you had bothered to stick around. How was I supposed to tell you? I had no idea where you were."

"Very clever, trying to turn this on me. I knew you'd

do that. But it won't work. Because I have a little something that you want now, don't I?"

"Don't you dare hurt her, Brody."

"What did you do with the money, Holly? You're out there living your best life while I work myself to the bone to barely get by? You're probably living in Hollywood. Are you kidding me?"

"I wasn't living my best life. California is expensive. I'm barely getting by, too."

"You're a liar!" He was shouting now, which was the last thing Holly wanted Georgia to hear.

"Please, Brody. Don't yell. You'll scare her."

"The way I see it, you owe me. Georgia is half mine, and you owe me at least half of what she's worth."

It took Holly a moment to decode what he was trying to say. It didn't make sense. "You want…money?"

"I want five million dollars," he said, the amount sucker punching Holly in the gut. She opened her mouth but couldn't speak. "Five million, in the next twenty-four hours."

"Brody—she didn't make anywhere near that amount."

"She will."

"But I can't give it to you if I don't have it."

"Then I guess you don't get her back."

"Brody, be reasonable. This is impossible. It's a ridiculous amount of money that doesn't exist."

"Oh, it exists. Guess you just have to find it. And no police. If I so much as sense a police officer, this won't end well."

"Please. Just meet with me. We'll talk. We'll talk about money. I promise. I'll be fair."

There was a pause. Then, low and menacing, he growled into the phone. "I'm not interested in talking. If I don't get five million in the next twenty-four hours, I will raise her myself. She'll be worth five million in no time. And I won't be sharing anything with you. Because you'll be dead."

Holly went cold. She knew Brody Shipley. She'd been on the receiving end of his anger too many times to count. Brody didn't make empty threats. "Brody, I can't…"

"Five million in twenty-four hours, Holly. Or I will kill you."

The phone went dead.

THREE

All the color had drained from Holly's face. She gripped the phone until her knuckles whitened. She was talking about money, about not having it. The hair on the back of Ryan's neck stood up, just as it always did when his instinct told him someone was in danger. He still wasn't quite sure what was going on, but whatever it was, it wasn't looking good. If Ryan didn't know any better, he would swear this was a ransom situation. Surely Brody hadn't kidnapped his own daughter for a payout. None of this was adding up.

"But I'm telling you I don't have… Hello? Brody?" Holly checked the phone screen, put it back to her ear, checked it again. "Brody? No, no, no, no, no."

She redialed, and when it went straight to voicemail, she redialed again.

"Come on," she said, and then repeated in a yell, "Come on!"

Ryan touched her shoulder. His focus sharpened. "Holly?" he asked gently. Rather than respond, she just kept redialing. "Holly," he repeated. "What's going on? What was that phone call?"

She ducked away from his grip—a move that he tried not to take personally but felt all the way to his core anyway—and spun in circles, looking for something in the carnival crowd. A growing number of people were gawking.

"Where is he?" she muttered. And then she yelled, "Where are you? Brody!"

Brody Shipley. After nearly a decade without even thinking about that guy, here he was again, taking up real estate in Ryan's mind, and Ryan didn't like it at all. But at least Georgia was with her father, not a stranger. That had to be a positive sign, right?

"Okay, so we know for sure she's with her dad," he urged.

Finally, Holly's attention allowed him in. "She's not *with her dad*," she said. "Her dad has had nothing to do with her for two years. She's only five. He's basically a stranger to her." She swiveled to talk to Georgia's little friend, who was still standing nearby, her thumb in her mouth. "You said she talked to him?"

The little girl nodded solemnly.

"Did it seem like she knew him? She recognized him?"

The little girl nodded again.

"Did she seem scared?"

The little girl shrugged.

"I don't understand." Holly paced a few steps, pushing her hand against her forehead. "How did he even know I was in Garnett?"

"Small town," a nearby woman offered. "Everyone knows everything."

Not true, Ryan thought. *They don't know everything. There are some things about me that only I know.*

But Ryan let that thought go, unwilling to allow himself to get distracted.

"So he was planning this all along," Holly said, more to herself than to anyone else. As an officer, Ryan had seen panic more times than he could count. He knew that his calm confidence was often a comfort for them. But none of those people were Holly. This felt so much more personal, and his stoicism was slipping. "He was stalking her and planning when to make his move. I practically handed her to him." She gazed around the carnival. "They could be anywhere. What do we do?"

Ryan wasn't in uniform, so he didn't have his radio. He grabbed his phone. "I'll call it in. Get carnival security to do a little searching, maybe shut down the exits, get some officers on the lookout."

Holly grabbed his hand to stop him from dialing. "No. No police. He said no police."

"I'll tell them to keep it low-key. He'll never know."

"He said no police," she repeated, her voice wavering. Ryan could see that she was on the edge of breaking down.

"Holly," he said gently. "Every second that goes by lets him get farther away. If they leave this carnival, they could go just about anywhere. If we can stop him here, or somewhere nearby, that would be best for everyone. Especially for Georgia."

"He said no police," she repeated urgently. "No police—or he will kill *me*. And he'll do it, Ryan. He'll kill me without thinking twice about it. What kind of life would Georgia have then?" She looked up at him with those huge, blue eyes that he'd been powerless against since he was twelve. "Please, Ryan. He won't go far because he's expecting money. We'll find him." Ryan still hesitated. "Please. Give me an hour. If he doesn't turn up by then, we'll call the police."

He hated everything about this. The chances that Brody would be stopped and Georgia would be found without the help of police were slim and getting slimmer with every tick of the clock. An hour was an eternity in kidnapping situations. He knew the statistics around parental kidnapping. He knew that about 40 percent of parents in these cases didn't get police involved, but he also knew that about 20 percent of parent-abducted children went missing for a month or longer. He doubted there were really any statistics about parental abductions of famous children. He wasn't as convinced as Holly was that Brody would stay nearby, that he wouldn't do anything rash, that he only wanted money and would simply return their daughter once he got it. Georgia was a commodity worth way more than five million dollars, and Holly was just being hopeful.

But he could never say no to Holly.

He slipped the phone back into his pocket.

"Okay," he said. "But we're wasting time standing here. We need to look around. Ask if anyone saw them. And we need to do it quickly."

She nodded. "Let's split up and meet back here in five minutes."

"I can help," a nearby woman said, stepping forward.

"Me, too," a man said, handing the infant he was holding to his wife.

"We'll take this little girl back to her parents," his wife said. "Can you show us the way, sweetie?"

There were murmurs of "I'll help, too" from around the small crowd that had joined them, and Ryan could see Holly becoming overwhelmed. He stepped closer to her, put his hand on her back and leaned down to talk to her, quietly, gently.

Even in this crisis moment, he was aware of the scent of the shampoo in her hair—something flowery and clean that took him back.

"The more people looking, the faster we will find her," he said. "None of them are police."

She hesitated, then nodded. "Okay. Yeah." She raised her voice. "Her name is Georgia. Blond hair, blue eyes. She's wearing a pair of jean shorts and a teal T-shirt with a…a sparkly fish on it. And sandals. She's wearing sandals. And…and carrying a white, stuffed cat. Here." Her hands shook around her phone as she pulled up a photo from the weekend before and held it face out for everyone to see. "This is her. Please—no police. Do not call the police. If you see her, call me." She rattled off her phone number, and people dutifully tapped it into their phones. "And please don't post any videos online. You will jeopardize Georgia's safety."

The crowd dispersed, with Holly in the lead. Ryan lagged behind, doing what he did best. He was an information-gatherer, an observer. He liked to take a moment—even if it was just a few seconds—to assess a situation before he made any sort of move. In his earliest days as an officer, he would have offered up a quick prayer for strength and guidance and the courage to follow his intuition.

But after the breakup with Morgan, Ryan and God weren't exactly on speaking terms. Strength and guidance weren't two gifts God had been offering him lately.

He decided to forgo the prayer and just study the carnival, which seemed to have resumed its manic merriness despite the tragedy that was unfolding within its boundaries. Save for the half dozen people who were with Holly, even the people who had come out of the hay maze to watch the situation unfold had begun to drift back to their fun, not wanting to get involved.

People had such short attention spans for the unpleasant.

Sometimes that was a good thing; sometimes it was astonishingly cold. Right now, it was a little of both. Ryan was able to see the carnival more clearly, hear the bells and the mechanical roars and the squeals of delight, take in a whole picture.

Brody was smart, taking her from a carnival. They could be just about anywhere, and nobody would know it. And the fact that Brody had thought this through scared Ryan most of all.

Holly was shaking to her core. This couldn't be happening. Not to her. She'd been so careful. She'd come to Garnett to protect her daughter. She'd never had any thought that the danger could actually be in Garnett. Forget creepy strangers on doorsteps asking for locks of Georgia's hair—they were nothing compared to the child's own father.

Five million dollars. Five million!

She was terrified. And outraged.

Did Brody really think they would pay Georgia that kind of money for a few small scenes in her first movie? Absolutely not. And even if they had, Holly still wouldn't have touched it. The Icefall thing was all about making sure Georgia had a future that looked different from Holly's. There was no way in the world that she would give that money to Brody.

Five million. The number tumbled around in Holly's head like clothes in a dryer. *Five million, five million, five million.*

Where on earth was she supposed to get that kind of cash?

It wasn't the first time someone had assumed that Georgia was insta-rich after the *Precipitators* movie blew up the box office. Even she, in her past, might have assumed that Georgia's fortune was much bigger than it was. *What are you doing here?* had been the question she heard most often when she'd shown up for work the day after the movie's release. *You don't have to work anymore. You're rich!* As if she'd put her daughter to work so that she wouldn't have to. You learn a lot about the people in your life when celebrity happens.

Granted, the movie did very well, and Georgia was getting a nice bonus. Not to mention the offer for the second movie was likely to be higher than the first one had been, given the public's love of the Icefall character. And then there would be commercials and residuals and…a future. But, for now, Icefall's "windfall" was nothing to fall over about.

Holly stopped in her tracks. The second movie was undoubtedly going to offer a higher payday than the first. She had been hesitant to sign the contract—her reluctance was why she was in Garnett in the first place—but maybe she could drive the offer up and get them to wire her a deposit. Maybe she could get her hands on five million dollars.

But could you do all of that in a day, Holly? Do you really want Brody to have her any longer than absolutely necessary?

No, of course she didn't. But she had to do everything she could, and one thing she could do was get as much of the five million he was asking for as was humanly possible.

She stopped, pulled up her messages and fired off a quick text to Georgia's agent, Lynne, who had been pressuring Holly to sign the contract.

Ready to talk deal. Want more $.

Instantly, Lynne responded:

Great choice! Will see what I can do.

Ordinarily, the pit in her stomach would be because she was unsure about signing Georgia's life further into child stardom. But now that pit was overridden by the gnawing sensation when she thought of Brody's voice on the other end of that phone call. *Five million in twenty-four hours, Holly. Or I will kill you.*

Holly knew Brody. He didn't make idle threats. Her hand drifted to her opposite wrist as it often did when she was uneasy, rubbing where there had once been a severe break, courtesy of Brody Shipley. Panic welled up in her. She closed her eyes.

Deep breath, Holly. Deep breath. He never hurt Georgia. Not once.

She hadn't seen Brody for two years. Would she even recognize him if he wandered by?

Yes, she thought. You never forget the face of your abuser. Plus, you're looking for Georgia, not for Brody. Just focus. Look for her.

She opened her eyes again, and at first all she could see was light-haired little girls everywhere. Her heart stopped with every blond head that bobbed through her path. Georgia's name was perched on the end of her tongue, ready to be cried out, her muscles tense to leap for her, but then she would notice the differences—a nose too large, hair too wavy—and feel the frustration creep up her shoulders.

Like a needle in a haystack.

But then she took another deep breath to focus and looked harder. These girls were blonde, yes, but they weren't Icefall-blonde. They weren't Georgia. She knew Georgia better than she knew herself. Brody might manage to get by, unseen, but the chances that her daughter would slip past her were slim to none.

The ground churned beneath her feet as she darted

through the crowd, scanning, scanning, scanning. No Georgia anywhere. The time ticked away.

"Holly," she heard, and a jolt coursed through her as she whipped toward the sound of her name.

Brody.

But it wasn't Brody. It was Ryan coming toward her. Her heart sank, seeing that he was alone. A part of her had hoped that maybe he'd come for her because he'd found Georgia.

"She's nowhere," she said, hating the desperation in her voice, the way it made her actually feel more desperate. She gulped in a breath. "What do I do? They're just gone."

Ryan's jaw pulsed as he gazed around the area. Holly could see him processing, calculating, looking for clues. She knew that what he thought she should do was call the police, but she couldn't make herself do it. Not yet. "Think back to the phone call," he said. "Did he sound like he was walking? Driving? Was there wind? Crowd sounds? Running water? Any noises at all?"

"I… I don't know," she said. "I don't know."

"Think," he said, his voice reassuring and calm. "Take a deep breath and think."

Holly swallowed, breathed, tried to concentrate, even though her mind was racing and it seemed impossible. Just when she was about to give up, she heard Brody's voice in her mind.

Just listen. Whump. *For once in your life, stop talking and listen.*

"Wait," she said. "Yes. Yes! There was a sound after he told me not to talk."

"What kind of sound?"

"It was like a thump. Like a…" Her eyes widened. "Like a car door closing. They're in a car." She reached toward Ryan to steady herself, as her legs felt weak. "Ryan. They're not here anymore. They're gone. Georgia is gone."

FOUR

Holly's eyes swam with tears as she looked up at him helplessly. "How will we find them now?"

The truth was, he wasn't entirely sure what they could do without outside help. His instinct was to call it in, ask for backup and get officers on the road watching out for the car. Put everything he had behind it. That was the best approach to the situation. But Holly had already shut that down. Whether it was her past with Brody or his current threats, or a little of both, she was too frightened to consider it. Ryan had to trust her instinct. That made them the only ones who could be on the lookout.

"I don't even know what he drives, Ryan." She'd pushed her hands up into her hair, burying her fingers inside.

"It's a white sedan," he said, pressing his memory hard for a make and model but coming up with nothing solid. "I think it was a Ford, but I'm not sure. But I'm positive that it was white. And it had a dent in the back passenger door. Not from a wreck, but like someone kicked it."

Her mouth formed a straight line. "Brody likes to kick things."

Ryan was sure there was a memory behind that statement, but now was not the time to ask about it. He started walking toward the exit gate, Holly right on his heels. "You go back to the maze. See if anyone turned up anything there. Here, give me your phone." He took her phone and quickly tapped in his number. "Call me if you find out anything. I'll do the same."

"Back to the maze? I can't just stay here, knowing that she's not here. Who knows how far they'll get?"

"You can't afford not to be here if she turns up. Like you said, they won't go far. Not if he's expecting money. He's got to be hanging around Garnett. And if he is…" He paused, turned and looked Holly in the eyes. "If he is, I promise you, I'll find him."

Back to the maze. It seemed impossible. Holly's legs felt leaden, unable to be moved. She watched Ryan jog through the carnival gate and into the parking lot. Within moments, he was out of her sight. If it were that easy for him to vanish with her right there watching him, how easy would it be for Brody and Georgia to disappear? For Brody to decide that he wanted to simply raise Georgia himself after all? Forget about the money that she didn't have. Forget about the mess and danger of killing Holly. It was a big world out there; it was easy to blend in and start over if someone really wanted to.

But Brody didn't want to. He wanted in on the fame and fortune.

Holly seethed at the thought.

Does he think I won't notice if Georgia is suddenly in all the movies? That I won't be able to find her? No, he doesn't think that. He will kill me first. He doesn't mind danger, and he's not afraid of a mess.

She was transported back to the first night that Brody hit her. They were arguing about a frozen pizza, of all things. She'd left it in the oven too long. She'd giggled as she struggled to cut it, had joked that he should have married a better chef. When he'd slapped her, he'd done it with such force, she fell to the kitchen floor, skidding a few inches backward. She had sat there, still holding the pizza cutter in the air, stunned into silence—too shocked even for tears—and watched as he swept the pizza, pan and all, onto the floor, then stormed out of the room.

Later, he'd apologized profusely. He'd been hungry and stressed out about money. To him, a ruined pizza had meant not eating and not being able to afford to eat. It was irrational, but it was only because he loved her so much and wanted to give her everything and hated himself for not being able to. They'd prayed on it together. She'd forgiven him fully. He was on edge. He had been worried about her. He'd simply lost his temper.

Two things she didn't know yet at the time: He would *simply lose his temper* again and again until he literally broke her. And, by then, she was already pregnant.

But he never hurt Georgia. Never so much as mussed a single hair. Not that he'd doted on her and treated her like gold; he'd ignored her and pretended she didn't exist. Unless her existence somehow benefited him.

Which was the case today. In the scope of Brody's behavior, this all made perfect sense.

The hay maze came back into view and Holly stepped up her fast walk into a run. For the most part, people had forgotten about the scene that had just taken place there. A few parents had come back and were standing around awkwardly, talking to one another. They looked sheepish when she approached. She didn't need to ask, but she did.

"Did anyone find anything?"

A man shook his head. "Are you sure you don't want us to call the police?"

"I think it's time for that," a woman said, nodding.

Holly pointed toward the direction of the parking lot. She knew this song and dance well. Even if she told them not to call the police, they still would. They were well-meaning and didn't understand how abusers worked. "Ryan—the man I'm with—*is* the police. It's already been called in." A small lie but one meant to protect Georgia. "But thank you for the help."

The man shifted on the balls of his feet. "Some people are saying the little girl is from a movie?"

Holly sighed. She supposed she knew this was coming.

"Icefall? From the *Precipitators* movie?" he continued. "Is that true?"

Forgive me, God, for the lies.

She shook her head. "We hear that all the time. She's not."

He looked unconvinced. "She looks exactly like her."

"I know."

"Maybe that's why the man took her?"

You are so much closer than you think.

"He's her biological father. He took her because he wants to get at me." At least that one was closer to the truth.

Another woman approached, dragging a little boy along by the hand. "Did anyone find her?"

Holly and the man shook their heads. Holly watched the crowd closely for a sign of Brody or Georgia, even though deep down she knew that it was pointless. She knew that they were nowhere to be found. Not in the carnival, at least.

"Should we call the police?" the woman asked, and the lies started up all over again.

If I were Brody Shipley, where would I go?

Ryan screeched out of the carnival parking lot, spewing a shower of gravel out behind his car.

Bars? Not with a child. Someplace where I could blend in as just another dad out with his daughter, like the park? The zoo? Maybe. Someplace quiet and secluded where Georgia couldn't shout for help or be recognized? Much more likely.

But where would that be?

Ryan hadn't been back in Garnett long enough to revisit all the old haunts. He didn't remember the places they all used to go when they were teenagers. His mind had been occupied with other things, like getting settled in his new job, fixing up the old house, and…well, how it all went down with Morgan. And whether or not his mother had made sure everyone knew that her son had broken off an engagement with a beautiful, accomplished young cadet.

What was he thinking—of course his mother would have spent hours telling her friends about her heartbreak at losing *a dream daughter-in-law* and her worry that her only son would end up alone forever and she would end up without grandchildren. It was possible—probable, even—that more than a few people in Garnett knew that the girl Ryan had broken it off with was adorable, smiley, intelligent and kind. And it was true that Morgan was amazing. Ryan couldn't deny that. She was perfect in just about every way. Except for one. A really big one: She wasn't Holly.

Not that he was aware of that when he broke up with her. Not really. He just knew something about his feelings for her was off. And now that he was spending time with Holly again, it became crystal clear that the "off" thing about Morgan had everything to do with his inability to get over losing Holly.

But it was hardly lost on him that if he'd stuck it out with Morgan, he wouldn't be racing around Garnett right now, trying to remember old hangouts and hoping he wouldn't stumble upon a tragedy if he did, in fact, find Brody Shipley.

That was his worst fear, honestly. That Brody would do something to Georgia and Ryan would have to break the news to Holly. Holly seemed sure that Brody wouldn't hurt the little girl, but Ryan was less sure. He'd always seen Brody as a wild card. Of course

Ryan had been obligated to deliver terrible, tragic news to people before. Many times. But none of those people were Holly. It would destroy her, and in turn it would destroy him.

"White sedan," he said to himself as he peered through the windshield, looking, looking, looking. "White sedan." He wished he had paid attention to what kind of sedan it was.

His phone rang and he thumbed it on over Bluetooth.

"Find anything?" Holly's voice was tiny and breathless.

"Not yet. I take it nobody at the hay maze did, either?"

"No. They're going to keep looking. They have my phone number."

"And?"

"And I'm heading out, Ryan."

"Holly..."

"I can't just stay here and wait while he gets farther and farther away with my daughter." Her voice broke on the word *daughter*, ripping Ryan's heart around in his chest. Of course she was going to be fiercely protective of the little girl. He supposed he would expect nothing less from her. He heard a car door shut, and the wind cut out of the phone call. Holly's voice sounded clearer. "Where are you checking, so I can go to different places?"

"I'm just driving," Ryan said. "I have no idea where he might go."

"Ordinarily, I would say bars," Holly said bitterly. "But with Georgia..."

"Maybe bar and grills?"

"Maybe."

"Okay, I'll hit those."

"And I'll hit the secluded spots we used to go to."

So she remembered.

"Meet back at the house?"

"Yes."

Ryan took a breath and turned his car into a parking lot. No white sedan out front, but he supposed he should go inside anyway. Ask around. "Okay. Let's meet in thirty minutes. Or sooner, if one of us finds her."

Holly let out a shaky breath. "Not *if. When*. We will find her, Ryan. We have to."

FIVE

If she hadn't been so panicked, Holly might have felt as if she was taking a tour through her teenage years. She was surprised at how easily she could find the abandoned train depot pushed back behind a cul-de-sac, the loading docks of a strip of rarely used warehouses, the parking lot behind the movie theater. All the places Brody would go if he wanted to be alone.

Finally, she drove the winding roads that took her past the lake, checking picnic shelters, one by one, even though Brody always went to the same place: Shelter 9.

They'd had so many gatherings and picnics and fun times at Shelter 9. But it was also the shelter where he made her burn her journal, which she'd accidentally left out one evening when he came over. In it, she had expressed some doubts about him, about their relationship. She'd begun to question whether the forever that they were talking about was the best forever for her.

She'd felt so guilty when he brought it to her, eyes rimmed red as though he'd been crying, begging her not to fall out of love with him. She'd immediately offered to get rid of the journal, and he'd eagerly agreed, insisting that the best way to put this behind them was to burn it. They'd taken it to Shelter 9 and tossed it into the firepit. He'd brought lighter fluid and a lighter. She'd slowly ripped out each page and tossed them, one by one, into the fire, the entire time thanking God that she hadn't written about her true feelings: that Brody couldn't be her forever future when she had such deep feelings for Ryan.

After they married and Brody began to show his worst, most controlling, side, Holly beat herself up for not seeing it that night—her thoughts and emotions literally going up in smoke because he had violated her privacy. She'd felt guilty, while he'd felt righteously angry. There was no room for her to consider that maybe she ought to be the angry one. Her journal was hers, not theirs. But, as always, Brody had consumed her, and she'd let him.

Pulling off the main road now brought back all those feelings of shame and regret and resentment, but they were cut short when she spotted a white car sitting in the parking lot of Shelter 9. Holly sucked in a breath. Her throat ached. Ryan had said that Brody was driving a white sedan.

It took everything she had not to simply open her door and jump out, hit the ground running. Instead, she pulled up behind the car and parked perpendicularly so Brody couldn't just screech away the moment he saw her. She got out of the car and hurried toward the shelter. There was no one inside, but she could hear voices coming from the woods where the brush butted up against the water.

——One of those voices was a child's voice.

Holly's heartbeat quickened and she had to hold herself back from calling out. All she could think of was wrapping Georgia up in her arms. She wouldn't even care if Brody slipped away, as long as she got her little girl back. She hurried toward the shelter, toward the voices, heartened by the curious, happy chirping of the child. She couldn't hear what was being said, but at least there weren't tears. At least he was giving his daughter that much.

Thank You, God, she thought. Thank You for helping me find her. Thank You for keeping her safe.

She slowed when she reached the shade of the shelter, suddenly unsure if she should burst through the trees and weeds or wait at the picnic table. Both would be a surprise to Brody, but which would give her the better chance of getting away? For sure, the shelter. It was closer to the car, which she just realized she had left running, the driver's-side door wide open.

But what if he were planning to do something awful? Georgia could swim but not well. She wouldn't be able to save herself if he were intent on keeping her under the water.

Would he do that? Would he drown his golden goose?

This was the scariest part of the whole thing— Brody was unpredictable. He'd been impulsive when they were married, but at least she'd sort of known him. Now, she had no idea what he was capable of or what he was willing to do. She never would have guessed he would go this far, so how was she to know how far he would truly go?

The voices got closer, and the weeds began to rustle, making the decision for her. They were coming toward the shelter; no need for her to sneak up on them.

Her phone buzzed in her pocket. She assumed it was Ryan, calling in to report what he had and hadn't found.

But when she looked at the screen, she could see that it was her mother calling, and that she'd missed multiple texts from her. The last one simply read 911.

She answered, but never got to say a word before her mother started talking.

"Oh, thank goodness you answered." Cheryl was breathing heavily, and there was a hitch in her voice. "What's going on, Holly? What's happening?"

Holly glanced at the brush, which was swaying with each footstep now. The voices were close.

"Mom, I can't..." she whispered, but then a blond child popped out into the clearing between the woods and the shelter, followed by a man.

Both were holding fishing poles.

The man was holding a tackle box in one hand and a small cooler in the other.

In front of him, a little, blond boy was stomping through the weeds in the cutest rain boots, proudly carrying a child-sized fishing rod, rambling about the size of a fish and how hard it pulled his line.

The disappointment was so instant and so intense, Holly's legs almost gave way. It was as though the world shrank into a tunnel, the sides of her vision gray and grainy. She was forgetting to breathe.

She'd been so sure it would be Brody and Georgia tromping through those weeds.

"Holly? Holly? Are you there? Did you hear me?"

The man spotted Holly and frowned, a slight hesitation in his step. He said something to the boy and then stepped in front of him. "Can I help you?" he called out. She could only imagine how she must have looked to him, disheveled and swaying.

Holly's mouth was open, but she couldn't answer either of them.

The man had stopped, the little boy peering at her from around the man's hip. "Hello?"

"Hello?" her mom echoed through the phone line. And then she said the words that snapped Holly out of her stupor and sent her flying back to her car, away from the shelter and toward home. "I said Brody was here. With Georgia. He took her things."

Ryan wasn't sure where to go. He'd cruised what had seemed like the entire town of Garnett and found nothing. Not a single white sedan, which seemed to defy odds. On any given day, he guessed he would pass a few dozen of them. He'd started to go back to the fair to cruise the parking lot one more time. Maybe the car was there and he'd missed it.

Even if it was, it's long gone now. Brody is smart enough to know that he can't hang around in one place with a kidnapped child.

That was the thought that scared him the most.

While he—and presumably Holly, at this point—were driving around searching for places where Brody might be hiding, Brody could still be on the road, moving, pulling farther and farther away from them. This was why it was important to get the police involved. Ryan's eyes flicked to the clock on his dashboard. It had been an hour or more. Brody could be halfway to Topeka while they continued to spin their wheels in Garnett.

His phone rang. Holly. He pushed the speaker button.

"Any updates?" he asked.

"He was at my house," she said. "My mom called. He walked right inside and went straight back to the guest room and grabbed Georgia's suitcase. When my mom asked why he was there, he shoved her out of the way, grabbed a few things out of the kitchen and left."

"And Georgia?"

"She was in the car."

"How did she look?"

He could hear the tears in Holly's voice. "My mom didn't get a great look at her but said she didn't think Georgia was crying or anything. But, you know, Georgia doesn't cry. Not easily. I'm sure she's confused, Ryan. I'm sure she's wondering why, all of a sudden, she's with him and not me, and why I didn't tell her he was coming to get her. She's little, but she's smart. And if she's still with him, tonight, at bedtime, she'll really know that something is wrong. She'll be scared."

"Just try to concentrate on the fact that even if she knows something weird is going on, she's not upset by it. She's going along with it. And she's not hurt. What about your mom? Is she okay?"

He heard a turn signal click and pop as Holly turned. "Mom says she hit her head when he shoved her, but she's fine. I'm going there right now. I don't know where else to go, Ryan. I've checked everywhere he might be." She took in a sharp breath, as if she suddenly realized something. "Except one place. His sister's house."

"Brenda?" Ryan hadn't thought about Brenda Shipley in years.

"Yes. Does she still live there?"

"I don't know," he said. "But there's one way to find out, and it's worth a try. I'll meet you there."

Ryan whipped the car around and headed back the way he'd just come. Their senior year, Brenda had surprised everyone by dropping out of school, marrying a much older man, and moving into his house off the highway. The house was falling down around their ears even then and was part of no neighborhood—all the other houses around it having been torn down years ago to make room for progress. Somehow, Brenda's husband had resisted selling out to the city, and his house was separated from the world around him by a chain-link fence. A small oasis of junk and garbage and feral cats amid fast-food restaurants and grocery stores and used car lots.

Part of him was surprised to see that the place was still standing. He pulled up at the exact moment that Holly did. He could see an awful mixture of hope and terror on her face as she took in the same important detail that he did—there was no white car anywhere to be found.

Still, they both parked and walked up the crumbling sidewalk. There was a new addition to the dilapidated yard: toys. Children lived here now, a realization that made Ryan hopeful that this meant Brenda was still around, but also saddened that children were growing up in this mess.

They climbed the splintering porch steps and rang the doorbell. Instantly, what sounded like multiple large dogs charged the door, their toenails skidding on the floor and their paws thumping and scratching against the wood. Holly and Ryan moved back a step. He'd learned over the years that when you approached the door of a house with dogs, you never knew what might pop out at you when the door opened.

If the door opened.

His mind revved back into what-next mode as he began to consider the possibility that nobody was home. But just as he was turning to Holly to suggest they go back to Cheryl's house, the front door swung wide, the dogs separated from them by only a storm door. Brenda peered out at them through the screened top half of the door.

Brody's sister appeared as Ryan remembered her, except she looked like she'd aged thirty years instead of seven. Her face sagged, as if she were carrying around a weariness that was cell-deep. She squinted at him, and then her eyes turned to Holly. In the matter of milliseconds, her face registered surprise, then confusion, followed by disgust.

"What do you want?"

Holly deflated beside him. He imagined that she was

thinking the same thing as him—if Brenda was surprised to see her here, then she didn't know anything about Brody and Georgia.

Which meant she would likely have no idea where they could be.

"Have you seen Brody?" Holly asked, trying to ignore the still-barking dogs that were lunging toward the door.

"Why would I tell you if I had?" Brenda started to step back and close the door. "I don't owe you anything, and neither does my brother."

Holly jumped forward, causing one of the dogs to lunge against the glass with a snarl. "No! Brenda! Please. Don't close the door. I need to know if he's been here. It's important."

Brenda paused. "I heard you were back in Garnett. Sure didn't take you long to try to mess with Brody. The last thing he needs is you back in his life. But he don't live in Garnett no more, so you wasted your time."

"I'm not trying to be back in his life."

Brenda tipped her head to one side skeptically. "You just taking a poll then? Is that why you're here?"

"No, he's…" Holly swallowed, unsure if she could get the words out. Being in the presence of Brody's family again was hard and threatened to bring back old feelings of betrayal and abandonment. The Shipley family was as dysfunctional as a family could get. Yet they rallied around each other at every turn, making

Holly feel like she was the problem in her abusive relationship. If they didn't know where he was now, telling them that he had taken Georgia would likely only guarantee that the Shipleys would provide him with a safe haven to hide him from her. But she had to tell. She had to do everything she could. She wanted her daughter back.

And her life literally depended on it.

"He has Georgia," she said. "He…took her."

"Who's Georgia?"

"My daughter," Holly said, stunned. How could Brenda not even know her niece's name? Did Brody care that little? *"Brody's…daughter."*

Brenda frowned, as if she were trying to discern whether or not Holly was telling the truth. "So you're upset that he took his own daughter somewhere?"

Irritation rose in Holly. "No, he didn't *take her somewhere*. He kidnapped her. He hasn't been around for two years. She doesn't know him at all."

"Have you seen them?" Ryan asked, his voice sharp, cutting to the chase. Holly guessed that he was thinking the same thing she was thinking—there just wasn't time for this runaround.

Brenda squinted at him, then chuckled. "Ryan Oldham. I heard you were back in town, too. Ya'll just couldn't stay away, could you? Big, wide world outside of Garnett." She crossed her arms. "You brought a cop to my house, Holly? Same old, goody-goody tattletale that you always were."

"I'm just a friend helping out," Ryan said.

It had been a mistake to bring Ryan with her. Brody had specified no police, yet here Ryan was at his sister's house, asking questions.

"Nope," Brenda said, shaking her head exaggeratedly. "No such thing as *just a friend* when the friend's a cop."

"Ryan," Holly said, putting a hand on his arm. "Why don't you go back to the car?"

Holly sensed that Ryan didn't trust this situation at all, didn't trust Brenda and surely didn't trust Brody. He lingered, half turned, then shrugged and walked back down the porch stairs and across the weed-dotted sidewalk toward his car. Holly guessed, though, that he didn't get inside, but was standing next to it, at the ready.

"Listen," she said. "I don't know if you and Brody talk much…"

"Try never."

"Same here. That's why it's so important that I get Georgia from him. He's barely more than a stranger to her. If she remembers anything about him, I guarantee it's not much." This had been a fact that had made Holly hopeful and grateful. Georgia didn't remember witnessing the abuse, at least not on the surface. "I need to get her back. Please. One mom to another?"

Brenda let out an aggravated sigh, but released the tiniest bit of tension in her posture, which relieved Holly immensely. "I would help you, but nobody in our family has heard anything from him since probably farther back than you did. He left Garnett and that was that. I didn't even know he was in town. And I guarantee if I didn't know, our mother doesn't know. She would have called me immediately, if I didn't hear her shouting all the way from here. He stole a bunch of money from her. She doesn't want anything to do with him."

Tears teased Holly's eyes. With every dead end, her hopes were more and more dashed, as if God were only selectively hearing her pleas. If his family hadn't even heard from him, he wasn't planning on hiding out here.

"Can you think of anywhere he might have gone?" she asked.

Brenda shook her head, and Holly thought she could actually see some sympathy in Brenda's eyes. "I'm sorry, but I just wouldn't know."

"Okay," Holly said. "Can I give you my number? In case he shows up?"

Brenda hesitated, then reached into her pocket and pulled out a cell phone. She woke it up and handed it to Holly. Holly typed her number into the contacts and handed it back.

"I don't get it," Brenda said, taking the phone and shoving it back into her pocket. "What's he want her for, anyway, if he hasn't had anything to do with her?"

"Money," Holly said.

Brenda smirked and nodded. "Sounds like Brody. No offense, but you don't look like you've got money to give."

"I don't," Holly said. If Brenda didn't know about Icefall, she wasn't going to be the one to tell her. If memory served correct, Brody wasn't the only money-hungry Shipley in the bunch. It was a trait they all shared. "Please call if you hear anything at all? Even if it doesn't seem important?"

"Sure."

Holly turned and made her way down the porch steps. Ryan was still standing by the car, on alert.

"Hey, Holly?" she heard at her back just as she hit the sidewalk. She turned. Brenda was hanging out the front door. "It's a white Ford Fusion. An older one, like six or seven years old. Got a dent in the fender. He stopped by early this morning to pick up a sleeping bag and some clothes. He didn't say boo to me about anything, especially a kid, but it sure seemed like he was planning on leaving town for a bit."

So Brenda had been lying about not seeing Brody. Holly wondered if everything Brenda had told her was a lie. If Georgia and Brody could be inside that house right at that moment. Part of her wanted to shove through Brenda to find out for herself. But there were those dogs.

And the fact that Brenda was sharing information made Holly think he probably wasn't inside.

"Thank you," Holly said, filling with dread at the thought of Brody taking Georgia out of Garnett altogether.

"If you find him, tell him he still owes me that hundred bucks."

"Sure. I will." Holly turned and continued down the sidewalk. "How fast can you pack a toothbrush?" she asked Ryan as she paced past him and got into her car.

The thought of chasing down Brody by herself terrified her.

But the truth was, even if Ryan didn't want to go, she was going.

If she had to face Brody alone, so be it.

SIX

All of the girls Ryan dated after Holly ran off had one thing in common: stability. They were predictable. Deliberate. Content.

Morgan was always there. Always waiting for him with a smile and an itinerary. Patient and serene and certain. One thing he could be assured of: she would never blindside him, sweep the world out from under him, leave him holding empty hands to the sky wondering what in the world just happened and how he would take his next step.

In other words, boring.

He could give himself a million excuses for why he and Morgan would never work out, but in the end, he knew that her lack of spontaneity was part of what drove him away.

But racing through his house, shoving essentials into a backpack, he couldn't help wondering if jumping back into Holly's brand of spontaneity with no questions meant he'd given up on something.

Or had he gotten something back?

It didn't matter. He was going to help Holly find her

little girl no matter what it took. He didn't know if Brody Shipley was the kind of guy to make good on an ominous promise like the one he made to Holly, but if there was even the slightest chance that Brody might fulfill it, he had to stop him. And not just because it was Holly. Ryan had made a lifetime promise to stop guys like Brody Shipley. The guys who strutted through the world hurting whoever they could, however they could. The fact that it was Holly simply provided extra motivation.

He wasn't sure how much to pack. If he had his way, Brody would be in a holding cell by nightfall. But Brody had a few hours on them, and if she continued to tie his hands on calling for backup, it could take some time to catch up with him. Ryan threw some essentials into his backpack and shouldered it.

Holly was waiting for him by the car, a bag of her own slung over her shoulder. Cheryl stood on the sidewalk next to her, a soupy mess of tears and apologies.

"I couldn't stop him," Cheryl said when Ryan approached, not even waiting for him to say a word. "I didn't know what was going on, but even if I did… He pushed me." Her hand floated to the back of her head. Holly's frown deepened, her mouth set in a straight line, her jaw clenched. "I wasn't expecting that. Any of it. I was stunned, I guess. Like, physically stunned."

"Are you okay?" Ryan asked. "Do you need us to take you to the hospital?"

She waved him away. "No. No. I'm okay. Just rattled. You need to be out there looking for Georgia." Her voice choked in her throat again, and she burst out an anguished sob. "I'm so sorry, Holly. I should have stopped him."

"Mom," Holly said, placing her palm on her mother's back. "You couldn't. I wouldn't have been able to, either. I'm just glad you're okay. And I'm glad Georgia's…" She shook her head, unable to get the rest out.

"Did he say anything?" Ryan asked, trying to refocus the conversation. "Did he give any hint where he might have been taking her?"

"No, he just grabbed all her things, so it seemed like he was planning to leave town. But he didn't give any hint of where."

"Which direction did he go when they left here?"

She pointed. "He turned left, like he was heading for the highway."

Ryan didn't like the sound of that at all. The more time they gave him on the highway, the farther he could get. But he wouldn't go too far if he was expecting a big payout. But then again, this was Brody Shipley. Not exactly a rocket scientist. And he wasn't exactly in a rational state of mind right now, either.

Ryan knew that his best bet was to keep Cheryl talking. The more a witness talked, the more they remembered, and it was impossible to tell in the moment what tiny detail might become hugely important down the road. "Can you think of anything else he might have said? Anything at all?"

Cheryl wrung her hands together in concentration, but shook her head. "He just said that Holly was trying to cheat him out of the money he deserved, and he was going to get it back. I told him Holly would never take something from someone else, and he must be mistaken. And he said he saw with his own eyes what she was trying to hide when he and his friend Red watched that movie. He just kept repeating that she took what was his, she took what was his."

Holly's face reddened in anger. "He's the one who took from us. I could barely put food on the table while he was out doing who-knows-what, missing all the fevers and sore throats and bellyaches and bad days and mean critics and scary fans. And now—now!— he sees Georgia on some big screen and suddenly he cares? He wants to be a dad? And he has the gall to say *I'm* the one who did something to *him*? Absolutely not. Let's go, Ryan."

"I don't understand," Cheryl said. "This is about him wanting to be part of her life?"

"No," Holly said. "It's about him wanting her money. And he has no idea how much she does or doesn't have."

"He's asking for money?" Cheryl asked, glancing between Ryan and Holly. "How much does he want?"

"Five million," Holly said.

Cheryl gasped. "Can you give him that much?"

"Of course not. I don't have five million dollars. I'm lucky to have five dollars most days. Even if Georgia takes this next contract, she still won't have anywhere near five million dollars. She's a child actor, not Hollywood royalty. He's made this number up in his head, and there's no way I can meet it. We've got to go. Do you mind driving, Ryan?"

Ryan shook his head, dug out his keys and led Holly and Cheryl to his car.

"So what's your plan?" Cheryl asked. "If you don't have the money, how are you going to get Georgia back?"

Ryan tossed his bag in the back seat and sank in behind the steering wheel silently. He turned his key in the ignition and rolled down the passenger window where Holly and Cheryl were standing.

He wouldn't mind hearing Holly's answer to that question himself. Did she have a plan? Or was the plan to come up with a plan once they were on the road? Or were they just going to follow instinct until they found the girl? He hadn't really realized until just now, when Cheryl said it out loud, that they'd been just reacting. Reacting to the realization that Georgia was gone. Reacting to Brody's threats. Reacting to the knowledge that he had her on the road to nowhere.

Could they really get anywhere if they just kept reacting?

You tell me, his brain supplied. *Reacting is what got you back to Garnett in the first place. Maybe a little more praying and little less reacting and you wouldn't be so miserable all the time. Maybe you could let Holly go once and for all.*

Holly opened the passenger door and tossed her bag on the back seat beside Ryan's. "The plan is we're going to track down Brody, and we're going to get Georgia back, no matter what it takes. And, no, I don't know for sure what that looks like."

She climbed in and closed the door. Cheryl laid her hands on the window opening, curling her fingers around the top of the door, and leaned in. "Just be safe.

Brody seemed desperate, so watch out. I'm afraid he could be dangerous in that state of mind."

"He's dangerous in any state of mind," Holly said. She nodded at Ryan, which he took to mean he should get going. He put the car in reverse and Cheryl stepped away from the window.

Ryan peered through the passenger window. "Let us know if you think of anything else at all that he might have said, done, taken. Anything."

Cheryl nodded.

"And if he contacts you again, don't call the police, okay?" Holly added. "Call us."

Cheryl nodded again but seemed less certain this time.

"Let's go," she said, and Ryan rolled away, heading straight for the highway. It wasn't until they turned onto the off-ramp that Holly spoke again. "And Brody's the one who'd better watch out now."

The nerve of Brody Shipley acting like some sort of victim. Holly silently seethed as the miles rolled away, clenching and unclenching her fists, glaring into every car they passed, just in case he might be in one.

Ryan was silent beside her, but his questions hung unsaid in the air. He was hesitant. She didn't blame him. Who wanted to get in the middle of something like this? Nasty and fraught and full of history that wasn't his own.

In the end, she wasn't even the one who left. That was what really infuriated her. She stuck it out, all the way until he decided he didn't want her anymore. Until he'd found another woman's doorstep to darken. And then Holly was left feeling abandoned and scared while also feeling like a fool who didn't care enough about herself to get out of an abusive relationship.

She'd learned over the years that this was part of the hold an abuser could have on their victim—that the victim would take some, if not all, of the blame. She'd also learned to let that guilt and self-blame go. She was young. She was in love. She was trying to salvage some sense of family for her daughter.

In the end, look where that got her.

"You okay?" Ryan finally broke the silence.

She nodded, but then realized how ridiculous it was to pretend. "No. Not at all."

He nodded, as if he understood. And of course he understood. Because that was Ryan. That was one of the billion things that drew her to him in the first place. He was kind and gentle and understanding. He was a protector and a supporter and everything that Brody was not.

"It was always about her," she blurted. "Georgia. That was why I put up with it. Even when it was at its worst. I thought if I could just hang in there, maybe things would get better. I didn't grow up with a dad. I wanted her to have a dad around."

"But things never got better," Ryan prompted. "They only got worse."

Holly tucked inward as she gazed out the window, disappearing down a rabbit hole, through years, and into the worst night of her life, just one of many. "There was this one time. He had met a girl at work," she said.

"I knew it. She was, honestly, just the latest. He was always meeting new girls. I turned a blind eye, because I didn't want my jealousy to cause Georgia to lose her family."

"That's not fair to you. You weren't the one who was cheating. It wasn't you betraying the family."

"But it was how I saw it. I can't explain the mindset." Her voice trembled.

"You don't have to," Ryan said.

"Anyway, for some reason, I just couldn't turn a blind eye anymore. I don't know why. Every second he was at work just grated on me, because I knew he was with her. I knew he was happy when he was with her and probably really nice. And he was almost never happy when he was with me. And he definitely was not nice. I figured it was my fault."

"Holly…"

"I know, trust me. If I could do it over, I would do it differently. I would treat myself better and let Georgia see me be the right kind of strong. The kind of strong I eventually became. Just…let me finish." She took a deep breath. "So this girl. Tara. She worked the front desk at his office. And…and I don't know why I did it. I showed up there one day. Put on my cutest outfit and made sure I looked my absolute best, like Tara and I were in some sort of competition and Brody was the prize. And I put a big bow in Georgia's hair like she was a walking gift, and I made him a nice lunch and took it up there."

The images of that day flooded in on Holly, almost taking her breath away. She'd never told anyone about what happened. She had no idea why she was saying it now. Every word was crushing her chest, and every memory was smothering her. Guilt and humiliation and loss battered her from all angles. She'd thought that maybe going to all this trouble would show Brody how much she loved him and convince him to stop fooling around and get serious about his family.

She'd thought looking cute and bringing him a sandwich was going to change everything.

She was so blind.

"Tara was working, and when we came in the door, she knew who we were. Brody didn't carry photos with him, and he didn't have photos in his office, so I knew that she'd been in my house. In Georgia's house. And I wondered…had she been in there when Georgia was there? Had he brought her over while I was at work or shopping or something?"

Ryan said nothing. Just looked forward, listening. But the tension was building in his shoulders. His grip tightened around the steering wheel.

She took a deep breath. Now that she'd started the horrible story, she was determined to get it all out. "I got mad. For the first time, I wasn't sad or scared or sorry. I was angry. She was all smiles and happiness and talking to Georgia in a baby voice while we waited for Brody to come out, and I was standing there ready to boil over."

Holly would never forget the look on Brody's face when he approached the reception desk. He was open and friendly and almost looked excited as he walked toward Tara. But then his face changed when he saw

Holly standing on the other side of the desk, the baby perched on one hip. She understood then what it looked like when someone's face fell, because that's exactly what Brody's face did. It fell, sudden and drastic and dangerous.

"When he got to the desk, Tara said something— I can't remember what—something about how cute Georgia was or that she looked like him or… I don't know. I just remember she put her hand on his elbow and squeezed when she said it. Just—"

Holly reached over and gave Ryan's elbow a soft squeeze. The movement, in and of itself, was innocent. Could have meant anything or nothing at all. Ryan glanced at her hand, then returned to concentrating on the road.

But in that moment, watching Tara squeeze her husband's elbow, it did not seem like an innocent movement in the least. It seemed like…ownership.

"I don't know what came over me. It wasn't like me to put up a fight against anyone. But I said…" She paused, hearing those seven words that had haunted her nightmares for months after the incident. "I said, 'Get your hands off of my husband.'"

In that moment Holly recognized she'd made a grave mistake. She didn't even need to see the fury pass over Brody to know. She could feel it in the room. She'd become so in tune with his moods and when it was best to just pretend she didn't exist. His rage felt like a wet blanket stretching over her, smothering her. Or a storm cloud rippling with dangerous electricity.

She'd gone home and prayed, just as she always did,

for God to give her strength and help her get out of her situation. She prayed for the motivation to leave before he got home. She prayed for Georgia to have a better life to grow up in. She prayed for Brody to be sorry. For him to change.

None of those prayers were answered.

"He didn't eat the lunch I brought, of course. He wasn't even all the way in the front door when he threw it at me," she said. "He dropped in on me like a tornado. I was fixing dinner. Georgia was just waking up from her afternoon nap. I'd had all day to mentally prepare myself for a fight. But there was no fight about it."

"He hit you," Ryan said quietly. Not a question, but a statement. As if he were logging notes and wanted to get them right.

Instinctively, Holly wrapped her fingers around her wrist and rubbed. "He broke my arm in two places. He also broke the TV and the glass top stove. He kept shouting that he wasn't going to stop until I understood that I didn't own him and that I wasn't welcome at his work and that I couldn't talk to his receptionist like that. Receptionist." She scoffed. "He claimed that was all she was and that I was paranoid and delusional if I thought she was something more. I wasn't those things. He broke my wrist that day. And by the time he walked away from us for good, he'd given me two more concussions and broken my pinky finger so badly I had to have screws put in it. And yet I never threw him out."

"Holly, I had no idea. I'm so sorry."

"Don't. Don't do that. I feel foolish for letting it go

on so long. What happened to my self-respect, you know? What kind of role model was I being for Georgia? And even today—right now—I'm making myself feel better about what he's done by reminding myself that at least he never hurt Georgia. What on earth makes me think he wouldn't start now? Start today?"

"Don't do that to yourself," Ryan said. "If you start thinking he could be hurting her, you'll go crazy."

"Maybe I need to go crazy. Maybe that's long overdue."

He nodded thoughtfully. "But you have to remember, she's his cash cow. He's not going to hurt her, because in his mind, she's bringing him millions."

"I suppose you're right." She was sitting forward, tense, and pressed herself back farther in her seat. They passed a rest stop; she scanned every car, looking for a white sedan. But the cars were a blur of color speeding by her window. Not a single white sedan to be found.

It was like her prayers had finally been answered—Brody stopped abusing her—but they came with a huge asterisk.

Be careful what you wish for.

He stopped abusing her because he disappeared. And his disappearance led to Georgia's eventual rise in stardom.

And now she was gone, too.

Ryan didn't need to be told that Brody had abused Holly. On some level, he already knew it or at least could have guessed it. But hearing it out loud—hearing her say the words—felt like someone was sitting behind him fanning, fanning, fanning flames.

He hated the idea of Holly being hurt and afraid, and him not there to protect her.

She should have never been with Brody in the first place. Ryan should have confessed his feelings before she ever ran off.

Fear. Fear of rejection and fear of losing her friendship were what kept him silent. And knowing that he'd been ruled by those fears angered him almost as much as hearing about what Brody did.

How dare Brody find himself a diamond like Holly, and then treat her like dirt?

"You know what's really ironic?" Holly asked. "I prayed and prayed for God to somehow get me out of that relationship. And then Brody left. My prayers had been answered. Yet I wanted him back."

"You loved him," Ryan said, even though the words burned hot and traitorous coming out of his mouth.

"I thought so," she said. "But mostly I was scared to try to do it on my own. I had a paycheck that wouldn't cover the bills. No real skills. I was afraid of my own shadow. And I had this toddler to care for. And she missed him. Cried for him all the time. It was heartbreaking. She would cry and I would cry and I would feel betrayed that she missed someone who was so mean to me and then I would feel guilty for thinking she shouldn't miss her daddy and we would just sit there being a mess while he moved on with his life."

"So what happened?" Ryan asked. "You said you

were afraid of your own shadow. But you're not like that now. What happened?"

She gave a small, sad smile. "I had to grow up. For myself and for Georgia. I didn't want anything to do with dating, so it was truly just the two of us all the time. I never got a break. Until now. Ironically."

"So you got what you prayed for. You got out of the situation."

She shrugged. "Yes, but it sure didn't seem like an answered prayer. It seemed like punishment. It was a rough road. But I suppose God never promised us things would be easy, did He?"

Ryan knew what that rough road felt like. He'd prayed to forget about Holly. And that prayer had never been answered. He prayed that he would fall hopelessly in love with Morgan—the kind of love that would have him never looking back. That prayer also had not been answered.

But when he prayed for clarity, oh, he got that. He understood that life with Morgan was not his future. He also understood that the love of his life had married someone else. It was clear that he was going to end up alone.

He glanced at Holly. The setting sun streamed through the passenger side window and picked up the creaminess of her skin. Her hands worked a wadded tissue nervously. He could see the faint scars on her finger where the pins must have been. Somehow that made her fragile, tiny frame seem so much tougher. His heart bloomed and bloomed as he watched her. He knew that—just as if time had never been—he would do anything for this girl.

And he hated that.

Because he was still in love with her, but that didn't mean she was in love with him.

"In my experience," he said, "that's how prayer works. Randomly, vaguely and not exactly what you wanted. I've given up on that."

"Why would you give up?"

The urge to tell her everything came over him. To just confess his feelings for her, to tell her about how no woman could ever live up to her and that he'd prayed so hard for it not to be the case. He'd wanted to find Holly in another woman, but the hard truth was that no matter how hard he prayed, there would only be one Holly out there, and he had lost her to the worst guy. It was selfish, and he knew it, but at some point he had given himself over to her.

But he couldn't tell her these things. It was too vulnerable and not the right time. She didn't need the distraction of having to let him down easy, and even though this felt like a road trip in some respects, he knew it was very much not a road trip and they needed to focus.

"As a police officer, I've seen a lot of bad things happen to a lot of good people. Things that no amount of prayer can reverse. And it makes me wonder if it's worth praying. That's all."

She glanced at him, opened her mouth as if to say something, then closed it and went back to staring out the window. It was a long moment before she spoke again. "I guess I just can't give up on God," she said. "Even if I don't understand the answer, that doesn't mean He isn't listening to the request. Although… well…maybe lately I haven't been sure He's listening. But I guess I figure He's busy with someone else—maybe you—and He'll get back to me when I need Him."

"You make it sound like you've been put on hold with customer service."

Holly let out a weak sniff of laughter. "Sometimes that's how it feels. And right now, I really need to talk to the manager. My order's been filled with the wrong product."

Ryan chuckled. He wasn't sure how they could get to where they were from where they started or how they could be joking and laughing when they were trying to track down a monster who'd stolen Holly's child, but there they were.

"How did Georgia end up as Icefall?" Ryan asked. "Has she always been a child actress and Icefall was her big break?"

"Oh, goodness, no," Holly said. "They had a cute toddler competition at the grocery store where I was working at the time. It was a promo for baby food. And it came with a cash prize of $200 and a little blip of video on a commercial. I thought it would be fun and I really could use the $200, so I entered her. It was all a lark."

"And she won."

Holly nodded. "It was the hair. Everyone always goes gaga over the hair."

"You should know."

She chuckled, lifted a lock of her own hair and studied it, then let it fall back to her shoulder. "Yes, I do."

"So, someone saw her commercial?"

"Yeah. Weirdly enough, someone did. We were living in Kansas City, and some *executive* just happened to be traveling from New York to California, saw the commercial and asked around. And the rest is history. I just… Well, I haven't signed the contract for Georgia to make an appearance as Icefall in *Precipitators 2*."

"And this is why," Ryan said. "People coming after her fame?"

"This is why," she repeated. "Only I never thought that her biggest fan threat would be Brody. That's a little curveball. Exactly what I was talking about. The prayer has been answered—at least I think it has?— but I don't understand the language."

They rode along in silence, watching the trees zip by, silent hawks sitting on the tops, keeping an eye over the fields stretching off to each side. This was something Ryan loved about Kansas. The green and beauty and long stretches of solitude. A lovely woman sitting next to him, talking about important life things.

"Can I ask you a question?" Holly asked, breaking the silence.

"Sure."

"How come you never got married?"

And there it was, crashing through the beauty like a bomb. The one question he didn't want her to ask.

He was holding back. Holly could feel it. She'd laid her soul bare for Ryan and he was keeping his truth from her.

Typical.

Why did she insist on trusting men to be open and honest and safe?

"Never mind," she said quietly, turning back toward the window. She didn't need the distraction of this conversation anyway, even though she desperately wanted to know. "You don't have to tell me."

He didn't protest. So if it hadn't been clear before, it was clear now that Ryan was keeping something from her.

He popped off the gas and hit the brakes, slowing the car down with a lurch.

"There." He pointed toward a lonely gas station. "That's it. That's the car I saw Brody driving this morning."

He swerved onto the exit ramp. Holly's heart leapt, all conversation unimportant and forgotten.

She was this close to getting Georgia back.

SEVEN

Ryan barely had breached the parking lot before Holly opened her door of the still-moving car and lunged onto the pavement.

"Holly!" she heard behind her as she stumbled and fell, ripping a hole in the knee of her jeans. She barely even felt the fall, and definitely didn't care about her scraped knee. Her heart was hammering away in her chest—fear, relief, anticipation. Every possible emotion was coursing through her. She didn't know what she would say or do when she was finally face-to-face with Brody, but that was a detail she didn't need to think about. All she needed was to get her arms around Georgia. Then she would think about how to approach Brody.

She got up and continued toward the car, which looked beat-up and like it would barely run. She tried to imagine Georgia being secreted away in this rattle-trap, and a flood of gratitude that her daughter wouldn't have to get back in it again swept over her.

"Georgia!"

No one was inside the car, but Holly wouldn't be

convinced until she saw every nook and cranny with her own eyes. She yanked on the driver's side handle. Locked. She placed her hands on the window and peered inside. Nothing but empty soda cups and fast-food bags and wrappers everywhere. A filthy ashtray overflowing with who-knew-what kind of ashes. Windows so grimy it was as if she were looking through a shade.

And on the front seat, a white, stuffed kitten.

Holly let out a cry, yanked on the handle again, pounded the window with the flat of her palm and then moved around to the other side.

The door opened and she dove inside, sweeping up Kitty. Ignoring the garbage, she climbed inside, pulling up on her knees to peer into the back seat. Maybe Georgia would be hiding on the floorboard.

But she knew that wasn't true. Georgia would have recognized Holly's voice and called out for her.

There was nothing but more trash. She leaned over the seat and swept handfuls of it aside. "Georgia?"

"Holly." Hearing her name startled her, especially since it was followed by pounding on the driver's side window. She looked up, adrenaline tingles coursing through her body. Ryan. He pointed down. "Open the door."

"This is the car," she said, waving the toy. Somehow, saying it out loud made it truer. She wanted to cry. If Georgia wasn't in this car, she was inside the gas station. Either way, she was about to go back home where she belonged. And Brody was about to go to prison where he belonged. The whole world would be right again.

She flipped the switch to unlock the door and Ryan leaned in.

"She was here," Holly said, once again giving the kitten a reassuring squeeze.

Ryan seemed to be searching for something and then found it. He pressed a button and Holly heard the trunk pop open. Of course! She hadn't yet checked the trunk.

But if Georgia was in the trunk…and making no noise… The entire world turned gray. Holly hadn't checked the trunk because she hadn't even considered that possibility. She couldn't consider it.

Holly's throat constricted, her breathing coming in a thin whistle. "No." She started to back out of the car, but Ryan reached over and put his hand atop hers, both of their hands clamped around Kitty now.

"You stay here," he said.

"No," she repeated, and this time she really did feel like she might cry. "She's my daughter."

"Stay here," he repeated. He was right. If there were something horrible to be seen, she would need to steel herself to see it. She nodded.

He ducked out of the car and moved around to the back. He pulled open the trunk, blocking Holly's view through the back window. It must have been only seconds, but it felt like lifetimes to Holly. Finally, he shut the trunk, caught her eye through the window and gave his head a small shake. Georgia wasn't in there. Holly didn't know if she was relieved or disappointed. It would have been so much better if they'd found Georgia curled up in the trunk, alive and well, and just snatched her up and took her home.

Instead, they would have to face Brody.

Holly got out of the car, still holding Kitty to her chest. "I'm going in." She didn't wait for a reply; just trotted up the sidewalk toward the store. She could see, out of the corner of her eye, Ryan's hand reach toward his waistband and surmised that was where he wore his gun. She was reassured that he'd brought his gun with him, yet alarmed that their situation could come down to a gunfight in the end.

A blast of cold air swept over her as she opened the gas station door. A sleepy clerk watched from the counter, her chin resting in one hand. Holly plunged inside, trying to look everywhere at once.

"Georgia?" she called, choosing an aisle and rushing down it, past cans of Pringles and boxes of Pop-Tarts and batteries and motor oil and ChapStick. "Georgia! It's Mommy!" She turned the corner and raced down the next aisle and then the next. She'd swept the store in only seconds, and still there was no sign of her daughter. The girl was obviously there—Brody's car was outside, and Holly was clutching Georgia's favorite toy.

She must be in the restroom. Holly made a beeline for it, her movements bolder and faster as feverish alarm began to get the best of her. This was wrong. It was all wrong.

She plowed into the two-stall restroom and closed the distance to the first toilet in no time. She shoved open the door, which banged against the stall wall. Nobody. She pushed against the second door. Locked.

"Georgia?" She pounded on the door with her palm. "It's Mommy, honey. Open the door. You're safe now."

"What?" A woman's voice echoed back at her. At first, Holly just stared at the door, unable to make sense of why her daughter's voice sounded so deep and mature. She'd been that convinced she would find Georgia inside the stall. But then she peeked under the door and saw women's shoes, a woman's legs, and she knew.

Georgia wasn't in the restroom, either.

This made no sense.

She burst out of the restroom just in time to crash into Ryan, hurrying out of the men's restroom. He shook his head again. "Just one guy in there. Not Brody."

No. This wasn't possible. Nothing about this was possible. Her grip on her control weakened. She rushed to the bored clerk, who had moved to the end of the counter closest to the restroom and was watching them intently.

"Where is she?" Holly demanded.

The clerk blinked in surprise, her mouth opening and her shoulders shrugging.

"Where is my daughter?"

"I don't…"

"She's here somewhere. This is her cat. Where are you hiding her? Somewhere in back?" Holly spun on her heel, searching for a door to a back room. She didn't wait for an answer, but swept the aisles again. "Georgia!" she shouted at the top of her lungs. "Yell loudly so I can hear you!" The man Ryan must have seen in the restroom came out, looking confused. Holly swerved to avoid him, then barged inside. Georgia was small; Ryan might have missed her. She might have been hiding well. But a quick shove into the two empty stalls told her that he was right—Georgia was not in there.

The clerk was still standing in the same spot when Holly returned to the counter.

"Have you seen a child?" Ryan patted the air with his hand. "About this tall, blond hair. Four or five?"

"Five," Holly supplied. "She's five. And she looks just like Icefall, from the movies. Do you have her?"

The clerk's eyes lit up. "Oh! That girl. Yeah, she was here. I thought she looked familiar. Icefall. That's it. I was trying to figure out who she reminded me of."

Holly's heart felt as if it had stopped and then re-started again, double time. "*Was* here? What do you mean, *was*? Where did she go?"

"She left with some guy about five minutes before you got here," the clerk said.

Holly spun. Brody's car was still outside. "Their car is still here."

"What did they leave in?" Ryan asked at the same time.

The clerk closed her eyes tight as she tipped her head back to think, then opened them again. "Blue truck. Older blue truck."

Holly and Ryan exchanged glances. She knew that he must have been thinking exactly what she was thinking—*how was this possible? Did Brody leave a truck here for himself?* But, as if the clerk had heard them think the question aloud, she pointed out the window.

"It was that guy's truck."

She was pointing at the red-haired man who had been in the men's restroom and was now ambling down the sidewalk toward the white car.

"They met up and swapped keys. I remember now,

because the kid said something about a stuffed animal, and the other guy said they weren't going back to the car and she started crying. I thought that was real mean. How hard would it be to just go back to the car and get it? Is that it?" The clerk pointed at Holly's hand.

Crying. *Oh, no. Georgia, crying.* Georgia didn't do that unless something was really wrong. Holly's hand tightened around the stuffed toy. Whatever she did, she had to get Kitty back to her daughter.

The identity of the red-haired man from the restroom came to her. Mike Johnston, who everyone simply called Red, was a pal of Brody's from childhood. Brenda had mentioned Red, too. Of course Brody would call on Red. And of course Red would be willing to do whatever illegal thing Brody wanted him to do. Holly hadn't seen Red in ages. But he was about to be reunited with her, up close and personal.

Ryan was one step ahead of her. As soon as the clerk pointed to Red, Ryan sprang into action, whipping open the glass door in a blur—almost taking out a woman coming in from the pumps—and sprinting down the sidewalk.

Holly took off after him, weaving around the bewildered woman in the doorway.

"Hey, is she actually Icefall…?" she heard at her back, but she just kept moving.

Ryan reached the man as he was climbing into the white car and yanked him out by two fistfuls of filthy T-shirt. The man made a noise of surprise but didn't fight at first; just let himself be swept out of the car and back onto his feet.

"Where is she?" Ryan growled so closely to the man's face that his own breath blew back at him. He shook the man. "Where's the girl?"

The man's face was a freckled oval of surprise. His mouth opened and closed like a fish. He was shorter and slighter than Ryan and far less muscular than him. He felt more like a pile of clothes than an actual body. Ryan gripped tighter.

"Tell us where she is," he said. "You don't want to be involved in this."

Rapid footsteps pounded the sidewalk, headed toward him.

"Red!" Holly yelled, and the man gave a brief, terrified glance in her direction. Ryan didn't dare let go of the man, who had started to try to edge away. "Where did they go? Please!"

To Ryan's surprise, Holly's tone was much more desperate than angry. He was angry. He couldn't help it. Someone had hurt Holly and could potentially be hurting Georgia, and all Ryan wanted to do was hurt back. He knew that he couldn't—and if they caught up with Brody, he might struggle with holding himself back—but in the moment, he was struggling to squelch those feelings. Adrenaline. Anger. Aggression.

"I don't… I don't…" Red had begun prying at Ryan's hands, trying to get loose. "Let *go*, man, what is your problem?"

"You're lying," Holly said. "You do know. You probably also know that Georgia doesn't know Brody at all. She's scared." Her voice wavered. The truth was, they were all scared, Holly most of all. "He wouldn't let her take her kitty." She raised the stuffed animal helplessly. Ryan's heart broke for her. He'd seen this so many times in grieving parents. They would focus on something that seemed minor and unimportant to everyone else. Something that was normal for them. A smashed bike, a missed favorite meal, a forgotten stuffed toy.

"I really don't know," Red said.

"You do," Ryan said, pushing into him again.

"I don't! I don't!" Red had raised his hands in surrender. "I swear to you. Brody called and said he needed to borrow my truck. He didn't say why. I didn't even know he had a kid. I was surprised to see her."

"That's because she doesn't belong to him," Holly said. "He abandoned her two years ago. He gave her up. He can't just take her now."

"So you gave him a truck, no questions asked," Ryan said skeptically. "That's a lie."

"We traded!"

"This car's all dented up and trashed," Holly said. "Why would you trade for it?"

"We're…friends," Red said.

Ryan had been around enough criminals to know when one was lying. And Red was. Time was ticking. He needed to move this conversation along. He yanked Red away from the car and spun him around, pulling him off his feet enough so that he was tripping along on his toes. He couldn't let on that he was the police; he was going to have to intimidate in a different way.

Which was not really his style. Ryan had become a police officer to go up against brutes, not to be one himself. Red was a brute. Just not physically. He was toying with Holly just the same. Playing games.

"The truth!" Ryan demanded. "You've got one more chance."

"I am telling the truth."

Ryan reared back like he was going to hit Red. "If this is the way you want to play it—"

"Okay, okay!" Red's hands flew up again. Ryan let his hand return to the front of Red's shirt. "He told me he was going to get a bunch of money and would share some with me if he could borrow my truck."

"And where was he going to take it?" Holly asked.

"I don't know."

Ryan's internal lie detector went off again, and he shoved Red against the hood of the car—not hard enough to hurt him, but hard enough to get his attention. To remind him that he could hurt him if he wanted to. He leaned over him, causing Red to bend backward over the hood. Red winced.

"Fine. Fine. He was going down to the cabin. I figured he had to move some stuff or tear down some trees or something. I never thought he would be taking somebody's kid." Red's eyes widened and he gasped. "He's not trafficking her, is he? I don't want nothing to do with anything like that."

Holly let out an anguished little noise. Ryan guessed she hadn't even thought of this possibility until Red said it out loud.

"I didn't have nothing to do with that. I just gave him my truck. Temporarily," Red said.

"Tell us about the truck," Holly said. "It's blue. What else?"

"It's a 2019 Ranger," he said. "There's a bumper sticker on the back window—Gone Fishing. Got a little guy in a boat."

"License plate?" Ryan asked. Red paused. "What's your license plate number?"

"I—I don't know, man. You have yours memorized?"

"Anything else?" Holly interrupted. "Toolbox in the bed? Anything like that? Anything at all?"

Red shrugged, shook his head and started spewing sentences. "It's just a truck. I wouldn't have let him use it if… I mean, I need the money. I got bills. My wife is pregnant again and I already got three and my oldest needs braces. I got laid off. My—my boss, he was out to get me. I had to quit. That was six months ago. We had savings, but who has savings to get by for six months?" At this point, Red was throwing out every excuse he could think of as to why he would help someone who was up to something awful. Anything to extricate himself from Ryan's hands and from the situation. "A hundred grand would have changed my life. Of course I was going to give him my truck. You would, too. Don't tell me you wouldn't. Are you calling the cops? Don't call the cops, man. I got a record. If I go back to jail, my wife'll have to move again. We already got kicked out once."

He rattled on and on and Ryan knew they had everything useful out of Red that they were going to get.

Holly seemed to also know this, as she started heading toward his car, the stuffed toy still clutched in one hand at her side.

Ryan loosened his grip on Red but stayed hovered over him. This guy was largely innocent—a victim of Brody's lies and promises—but he was guilty enough that Ryan wanted to leave an impression.

"If I so much as see you again," he seethed, "you *will* go to jail. Got it? I'll call the police so fast your head will spin."

"Wait. You're not gonna call right now? For real?"

Ryan backed away from Red and followed Holly. She was already in the car when he got to it. He slid in, keys in hand.

"Ready to go?" he asked.

She nodded, sadly staring at the kitten. "We should get moving," she said. "We're right behind them."

EIGHT

They rode along in silence for a while, both of them surveying everything zipping by their windows with more intensity than before. Ryan pushed past the speed limit, the engine growling as the car ate up the highway. Unless Brody was driving like a maniac, surely they would catch up with him. And if he were half as smart as he thought he was, Brody wouldn't be driving like a maniac for fear of being pulled over.

Holly enjoyed the fantasy of him being pulled over. Of them riding up on him on the side of the road, Ryan getting out and talking with the officer and then both of them drawing guns as Brody stepped outside the vehicle with his hands raised.

Of wrapping Georgia up in her arms and whispering to her that everything was okay. That everything would be different now. No more movies. No more Icefall. No more paparazzi and creepy fans standing outside their apartment. Just the two of them and a tiny grocery store paycheck that was good enough because it had to be.

Because the alternative just wasn't worth it anymore.

She checked her phone to see if she'd heard from Georgia's agent yet. She hadn't. Her thumbs hovered over the keyboard as she tried to convince herself to pull the plug now.

Forget it, she imagined herself typing. No amount of money is going to be enough. Georgia is out.

But she couldn't quite get herself to let go of that possible payday, just in case this dragged on, and she needed it to get her child back. Once again, Holly's circumstances had trapped her.

"You okay?" Ryan asked, ripping her out of her thoughts.

"Huh? Oh. Yeah. I mean, as okay as I can be. You?"

He nodded but never took his eyes off the road. "I'll be better when we find that truck."

"I like that word," she said.

He flicked the slightest glance her way, then back to the road. "Truck?"

"No. *When*. Not *if*, but *when* we find it."

An exit ramp was coming. Holly could feel Ryan start to ease up on the gas, so they both could get a look, just in case Brody had pulled off again.

"We'll find it," he said. "I'm confident. We'll find her."

"You were tough back there," Holly said. "With Red."

"Sometimes guys like Red need to be reminded who's in charge," Ryan said. "It usually doesn't take much. They act tough, but they aren't. Guaranteed by this afternoon, he'll have a whole story for his friends about how he got into a fight at the gas station and the other guy backed off. That's how they get their toughness. It's not real. Besides, I figured if I didn't step in and press him, you would hurt him."

Holly chuckled. "I might have."

"Brody better watch out. And pray that I get to him first."

Holly gave Ryan's shoulder a tiny push. "Believe it or not, I don't like to hurt people."

Ryan let out a little sniff that Holly guessed she wasn't meant to hear. Once again, Ryan was holding something back. But she had no idea what.

They reached the ramp and Ryan slowed. Both heads turned toward the restaurant at the bottom of the ramp. There weren't many cars to be found, and only a handful of trucks, none of them blue. Holly would have been very surprised to see Brody pulled off already. They'd only just left the gas station, and he was likely to keep going as long as he could to try and put some distance between them. If they had pulled over, something was wrong.

Once they passed, Ryan hit the gas again, and they bulleted down the highway.

That little sniff was bugging her. Surely Ryan didn't think she enjoyed hurting people. She hated it. If it were easy for her, she would have already told the persnickety soup commercial director to take a hike.

Thanks but no thanks. Georgia has changed her mind. We are out of show business.

She sighed and let her phone sag into her lap.

"Do you think I like to hurt people?" she asked.

"Huh?"

"You made a little noise when I said I don't like to hurt people. Do you disagree?"

"I didn't make a noise."

"Yes, you did. You…scoffed." She mimicked the sound he'd made.

"I didn't mean anything by that."

This was the second time he was holding back on her and Holly was quickly moving from curious to annoyed to hurt. What wasn't he telling her? And why? Here she was, being the most vulnerable that she'd ever been with another human. Letting him in on her darkest hour. Sharing with him her shameful past of accepting abuse. Crying and raging in front of him. And he was keeping her out.

"No," she said. "You did mean something by it. What? Who am I hurting? Who did I hurt?"

"Whoa. Holly. It was just a noise that I didn't even mean to make. It was nothing."

"That's not true. There are things you're not saying."

"I'm concentrating on finding Brody and Georgia," he said. "I really don't even have time to think about anything else."

"We have nothing but time," she said. "The cabin is eight hours away."

And it's going to get dark. And we won't be able to see blue trucks off the highway if they're parked somewhere without lights.

And she would need a distraction, or she would go crazy with worry.

He hesitated, as if he were thinking over whether he wanted to stick with his story, and then let out a breath.

"Okay. You want to know, I'll tell you. I don't think you like hurting people, no. But I also don't think you necessarily know when you are. Because…you don't want to know."

Holly had a sinking suspicion that he was talking about Georgia. That she'd hurt her with all the child celebrity stuff. She'd suspected as much for a while now, but it stung to have it spoken aloud. The unspoken accusation was like a third passenger in the front seat of Ryan's car, sitting between them on the center console, ugly and raw.

She swallowed the emotion attempting to push up on her. "For your information, I am well aware," she said. "Just because I don't walk around with it on my sleeve doesn't mean I don't know. I've been sitting here trying to figure out how to fix it."

His eyebrows pressed down in the center. "How did you know? I've tried to keep it from being obvious. I didn't want you to feel bad."

"Well, I don't need you to make it obvious for me to know. And I feel bad about it every second of every day, and I don't know what to do to make it better. That's why I'm here, by the way. I came here to get the courage to just end it once and for all."

His frown deepened. He paused, slowed to peer off at another building in the distance. "There's nothing for you to end," he said with a chill in his voice. "It's all good. It ended when you drove away from Garnett."

Now it was Holly's turn to be confused. "But that's why I'm back. I've got to make the decision to sign the contract this week. I was so on the fence in California, where we're surrounded by so much…aspiration. I needed to get some distance and make my decision. But, of course, even bringing her here ended up hurting her. I'm aware of that, too."

His shoulders slackened. He dropped his head and chuckled before looking back at the road. "Unbelievable."

"What?"

"I wasn't talking about Georgia. I was talking about people here."

"What's that supposed to mean? I haven't even been in Garnett for seven years. How could I hurt someone if I haven't been around for seven years?"

He let off the gas, pulled onto the shoulder and gazed at her, head-on. "That's the point, Holly. You just took off. You never even looked back, much less came back. Some of us were left picking up the pieces."

"What pieces?"

"Me," he said incredulously. "I had a huge crush on you, Holly. And when you left, I was shattered. *I* was in pieces."

Holly sat stunned in silence, aware only of her own breathing, the hum of the idling engine and the soft sway when cars zipped past, too close to the shoulder. All at once, the memory of her crush on Ryan flooded her. The fluttering in her stomach every time he was around. The deep, ripping anguish when she would see him bring a girl home. The way her throat closed every time she wanted to confess her feelings to him.

"You want to know what I haven't told you?" Ryan continued, his voice softer, injured. "I should be en-

gaged right now. I dated the same girl for years. I loved
her. But I didn't love her enough. Everything about
Morgan was perfect. But she wasn't you. And even
though it had been years since I'd seen or heard from
you, I couldn't let you go. It was like you still had this
piece of me in your back pocket, and you didn't even
know it. But also you didn't care, because you had
Brody. I didn't begrudge you that. I wanted you to be
happy. I just never understood how he could make you
happy and I couldn't."

"He didn't," Holly said.

"But I didn't know that until now," Ryan said. "I assumed you were out there, living your dream life and
hadn't thought about me since the day you drove away."

*That's not true, though, Holly thought. I did think
about you. All the time.*

She wanted desperately to tell him this but still wasn't
sure if now was the right time. He was finally letting her
in…and it felt horrible. Maybe there was such a thing
as too much water under the bridge. A flood that could
drown them both if they weren't careful.

"My parents have given up on me. They've given
up on grandkids. They think I just can't settle down.
They have no idea how much I wanted to settle down.
I just…wanted to settle down with the wrong girl. The
right girl was out of my reach, so I chose no girl at all."

So many thoughts and feelings wanted to pour out
of Holly. Confessions. Anguish. Hope. Future. But all
she could find herself saying was, "I… I didn't know,
Ryan. I'm sorry."

"I know. That's why I never said anything." He

checked his side mirror, turned on his signal and pulled back onto the highway, punching the gas again, to make up for lost time. The sun had set, and evening was pushing in on them quickly. "At the time I thought you should have known. Like, it was so obvious. But looking back, I probably hid it pretty well and was expecting you to know things that you couldn't have. I was so scared of being tossed aside, I leaned into the friend zone. I'd rather have had you for a friend than not have you at all. Turned out, that was exactly what happened anyway. My friend moved away, and I lost her forever."

"Not forever," Holly said. "I'm back now."

Ryan gave a thin smile. "And I'm glad you are. And you don't have to worry. That was a long time ago. I'm not going to pine after you. We're friends. It's all good."

Friends. The term *missed the boat* turned over and over in Holly's mind. She had been blind and silly and had latched onto something seemingly safe over something wonderful. How ironic that Ryan and she were so in tune that they gave each other up. A perfect match, each assuming that the other was too perfect to want to be together.

"Anyway," Ryan said, "it was unfair of me to say you hurt people because you didn't want to know. It's probably fairer to say I hurt myself because I didn't want you to know." He gave a sardonic chuckle. "You know now. When it's too late."

It's not too late.

Holly wanted to say the words, but part of her thought he was right—it was too late for them. She'd been too hurt, and he'd been too closed off. And to come back together under these kinds of circumstances? It just wasn't the right time.

And how many times did it need to be not the right time for them to just admit that there never would be a time for them?

Her phone buzzed, startling her. She snatched it up and sucked in a breath when she saw the screen light up with Unknown Caller once again.

"Hello? Brody?" Ryan glanced her way.

There was a slight hesitation, and Holly was just about to say his name again, when she heard a tiny, familiar voice. "Hi, Mommy."

"Georgia!"

The desperation in Holly's voice ripped at Ryan.

"Georgia!" she repeated, and fumbled with the phone, rushing to put it on speaker. "Are you there? Are you okay? Where are you, sweetie? Are you hurt?" The questions were coming far too fast for the little girl to answer.

"Mommy!" Georgia's voice rang out over the speaker. She sounded fine. She didn't sound terrified or hurt or as if she'd been crying. She sounded like a kid at summer camp calling home to check in.

Holly's hands shook as she held the phone up between them at ear height. She was smart. Her instincts were good. Any other mother might have been so desperate to talk to their little girl, they might not have thought of putting it on speaker. They might not have cared if he heard.

He pulled over onto the side of the road again and shut the car off so they could hear better.

"Are you okay, honey?" Holly repeated.

"Yep. Guess what? Daddy was in the hay maze and he played hide-and-seek with us and then he got me some ice cream and now we're on an adventure."

"What kind of adventure?"

"I'm not sure." For the first time, Ryan heard the slightest bit of concern in Georgia's voice. And he knew that if he heard it, Holly definitely did, too. Her hand tightened around the phone. "Daddy says you can come with us, but you have to pay your own way. Do you have any money, Mommy? He says you know the price of a-mission." There was a mumble, and then Georgia corrected herself. "*Ad*mission. You should pay it. I want you to come, too. How much is it, Daddy?"

Holly closed her eyes and tapped the phone lightly against her forehead. A tear squeezed out from under one eyelid and slid down her cheek. She let out a shaky breath and put on a smile to make her own voice sound lighter.

"I plan to be there, sweetie. I can't wait. Where are we going, again? Tell me where Daddy wants me to meet you."

Ryan had to hand it to Holly. She was breaking apart inside, but nobody would ever know it to listen to her. She was exactly the kind of mom he'd always imagined her to be. Nurturing and beautiful. He hated that she thought she had somehow hurt her little girl.

"I'm not sure. The woods, I think."

"The woods? Are there a lot of trees around you?" Georgia didn't answer for a long time. Holly gripped the phone harder and brought it closer to her face. "Georgia? Are you still there?"

There was some muffled noise, as if Georgia was covering the phone while she talked to Brody. "Yeah, I'm here. Guess what else? Daddy's got fishing poles. He told me there's a lake and I could catch a big fish and maybe we would even eat it. Right, Daddy?" There was the slightest pause. Ryan heard mumbling from Brody, but nothing solid. "I told him he could go fishing with us sometime, when we go home. Do you think Daddy could visit us at our house, Mommy?"

Another tear followed the first. "Sure, baby."

"What?" Georgia asked, and then there was the muffle of the phone being covered again. She came back. "He said he's going to be around a lot, so we should get used to seeing him. He said he can even stay with me if you need to go away. Are you going on a trip, Mommy?"

Coming out of Georgia's mouth, it sounded so innocent. Which is what made it all the more chilling. This was a threat and Brody was trying to rattle Holly. And from the looks of things, it was working. Tears flowed freely now, and her hands were shaking so hard that if she hadn't been clutching the phone as if her life depended on it, she might have dropped it.

"No, baby, not without you." She was starting to lose her demeanor. Ryan put his hand on her shoulder and lightly squeezed it. "But it's so nice of him to offer that, isn't it?"

"Yep. Daddy's nice. Did you know he watched the Sipperators movie, and he knows all about Icefall? I've been practicing my lines and especially the ped-er-greem soup song." Georgia began singing. Ryan's heart broke. He was pretty sure he would hear that voice in his head forever. When she finished, she said, "We can eat tacos in Daddy's car. He says he won't get mad if lettuce falls in the crack on the seat. I can probably eat tacos in our car now, too. Right, Mommy?"

Holly let out a breathy little laugh. "Sure. We can eat tacos wherever we want. Did you have tacos for dinner?"

"No. We haven't had dinner yet. But I want tacos, so if we see tacos, we're going to get them. Daddy says there's a taco place coming up in…how far, Daddy? Huh?" Ryan guessed that Brody wasn't thrilled about Georgia telling them so much about their plans. Now he and Holly would be scouring parking lots of Mexican restaurants, too. "Hang on. Huh?" More covering the mouthpiece.

Worry began to etch its way through the car. Ryan could feel it rolling off Holly. She chewed on one fingernail and stared at the phone as if it would come alive if she just willed it hard enough. "Georgia? Honey? You still there?"

It seemed like forever that Georgia was talking to Brody. Ryan began to worry about the miles that they were putting between them, and if this, too, was part of Brody's plan. The sun had fully set, and they were cloaked in darkness, the only light the taillights of the occasional car that whooshed past them, causing their car to jerk and bump in the force of the breeze. He wanted to get back on the road, but he was afraid of missing clues in the ensuing noise of the moving car on the highway.

"Georgia," Holly said, more firmly. "Georgia. Talk to me."

"Are you close, Mommy?" Georgia asked.

"I think so," Holly said. "Pretty close. But you have to tell me where."

"Oh, good! Daddy, Mommy's close. Maybe she can have tacos with us."

"Yes," Holly said, desperation lacing her voice. "Yes. Where are we having tacos?"

"Where are we having tacos, Daddy? Mommy wants to know so she can meet us there. Oh. Okay. Hang on, Mommy."

There was more muffling, and then Brody's voice came over the speaker, loud and clear. "I've got to hand it to you. That was a good try. I should have known that if I let you talk to her, you'd try to manipulate it out of her. You were always so manipulative, Holly. That's your problem. Well, part of your problem, anyway. Manipulative. Whiny. Your boyfriend there has got to be sick of listening to you whine by now. It gets old, Holly. I should know."

Ryan ground his teeth together, desperately holding himself back from responding.

Holly swiped tears from her cheeks, her jaw setting. "Put Georgia back on the phone."

"Nah, she's done talking. Gotta save our battery, right, George? Don't want our phone to die." He put some extra emphasis on the word *die.* "We wouldn't be able to talk to Mommy at all then. She would never know where we were."

"Brody, please," Holly said. "We can figure all of this out. We just have to meet. Tell me where to meet you."

"Oh, that's a good idea, Mommy," Brody said. Ryan hated how overjoyed Brody sounded, as if he were thrilled that he was making Holly squirm and beg. "You're right—we should make this part of our hide-and-seek game. Georgia, would you like Mommy to play hide-and-seek with us?"

"Brody…"

"You would? Me, too. That'll be fun."

"Brody…"

"We'll hide first, right, George?"

"Brody, let me talk to Georgia again."

"Mommy, you're just so smart. Too smart for me."

"I'll bring you the money. I've… I've got it. It's right here. I'll bring it to you. Just tell me where."

"Okay, Mommy. You count first. Since this is going to be a long game, I think you should count to…hmm… I don't know…five million. Go."

The phone went silent.

Holly stared at the phone, as if it had simply glitched. It wasn't possible that Brody had hung up on her. She felt the lost connection with Georgia instantly and fully, as if a cord between them had been snapped. She could almost imagine Georgia floating away, a helium balloon out of her grasp, soaring to a distant unknown.

"Brody," she said, knowing that it was fruitless, but unable to think of anything else to do. "Brody. Georgia! Are you there? Come on, come on, come on." She punched around on her phone but the call was gone. She tapped Brody's picture to call him back. The call went to voicemail without a single ring. "No, no, no, no…" She tapped again. Voicemail again. "No!"

Brody had the upper hand, and he knew it.

He always did.

You're too smart for me.

That had been one of his catchphrases while they were married. Usually just before he got really dangerous.

You're too smart for me, Holly. Too smart for your own good.

She'd come to see it as a warning, which he also knew. He was warning her here, too. The disconnected phone call could not be mistaken for anything else.

Well, he could warn all he wanted. He was not going to keep her from finding Georgia. She would not give in to fear. She would not let him win.

She sagged, her phone in her lap. "She's okay," she whispered. "At least I know she's okay."

"She thinks she's on an adventure," Ryan said. "She sounded excited."

Holly nodded. She hated that Ryan got to hear Brody belittle her. It was humiliating. A secret that she kept for so long, she didn't know how to have it in the open like that and still survive. Yet she did. And Ryan wasn't going anywhere. His hand was still on her shoulder, the warmth of his fingers seeping through the fabric of her shirt into her skin.

Holly stared at the black phone screen, as if it might

light up at any moment. She didn't want to miss it if it did. "That's Georgia. Ever the optimist. That's why she keeps getting hired. She's so easy. Part of me wishes she was being a royal pain for him, you know? Kicking and screaming and whining. But that's not who she is. She just doesn't do those things. If she does, I know something's wrong." She sniffed. "The only thing is she's a chatterbox. And Brody does not like a lot of noise."

Holly tried not to think about the times he flew off the handle because she was asking him too many questions or talking too much—*burning his ears*, he called it. *Railing at him.* It was one of the things that would set him off. She didn't want to think about him launching into Georgia the way he used to launch into her when the noise got to be too much for him.

She couldn't think about those things.

He's never hurt her. He's never hurt her. He's never hurt her.

"Let's think about what we know," Ryan said, once again in tune with Holly, as if he knew what she needed before she knew it. "Red said he thought they were going to the cabin. Was he telling the truth or trying to throw us off? That's what we need to figure out."

"Okay." She bit her lip, thinking. "Well, they're still in the car."

"No sounds of turning or stopping," Ryan said.

"And they're on the highway," Holly added. "Which makes sense, because the cabin is in Arkansas."

"There are woods and water wherever they're going."

"Right. She said they were going fishing. And that

they'd cook and eat a fish if she caught one. And the cabin is on the lake."

"So he's planning to lay low."

"But he expects me to get the money to him in twenty-four hours, so why would he drive to a cabin that's eight hours away? I'm afraid that this is all a game and he's planning on just taking her and disappearing."

"Maybe he's planning on having this resolved before they get there. He's not thinking they'll actually make it to the cabin."

Holly nodded. "Which is possible, too. Brody is nothing if not impatient. You don't think he'll…"

"He'll what?"

Holly shook her head, trying to shake away the thought that had intruded. Even thinking about it sent icy shards of fear through her. "I don't think he would. That would be going too far, even for Brody."

"What would? Talk to me, Holly. What are you afraid he'll do?"

She shook her head again, but the words spilled out anyway. "If this does get resolved while they're still on the road, do you think he'll leave her on the side of the road? Or…" She swallowed. "Kill her?"

"No," Ryan said. "We can't think that way. We have to stay optimistic. For Georgia. She's his golden goose. If he gets the money from you, he's going to think there will be more to be had. He will want her alive for the next payout."

But he'll want her all to himself, Holly thought.

But she had to let that thought go, because with it

came an acknowledgment that there was at least a possibility that he would never let Georgia go, no matter how this turned out. "Well, it's not going to be resolved in the way that he wants it to," she said aloud. "We'll just have to catch up with them, either on the road or in the cabin."

"Tacos," Ryan said. "Georgia told you that Brody thought there was a taco place coming up soon."

"Oh. Yes." Holly scanned through her memory bank until an image popped up, nearly taking her breath away. Sitting at a picnic table outside a taco stand just off the highway. Grease dripping down her forearm as she giggled and hung on to Brody's every word. There was a time that they were happy. They were just two, they were running away, and they were in love. Happy. "Tim's," she said. "Taco Tim's. We used to stop there on our way down to the cabin. They are for sure going to the cabin if Brody's talking about stopping at Tim's."

"So we go to the cabin. Where is it?"

"Huddig, Arkansas."

Ryan punched around on his GPS and turned on his turn signal.

"I'd forgotten all about that cabin," Holly said. "How could I forget? It was a dump, full of spiders and garbage and rotting wood, and I hated when Brody would take me there. But it was his favorite place to hide out from the world. Whenever his conscience got the better of him and he disappeared for a few days, I would inevitably find him there. It makes total sense that he'd take her there. I just can't believe it's still standing." Holly tried to stave off a mild burn in her gut at the thought of Georgia being inside some ramshackle building at the moment it decided to give way to gravity. "It was practically falling down around our ears the last time I was there."

"Maybe they've fixed it up," Ryan said, checking his mirrors for traffic.

"Or maybe he thinks it's a perfect place to hide, because who would suspect a little girl could be living in a heap of fallen-down boards?"

The traffic was clear, so Ryan darted onto the highway, a shower of gravel dinging the floorboard beneath Holly's feet. Back on smooth ground, he gunned it, the force of his speed pressing Holly back into her seat. A strange and complex feeling of being both off-kilter and the most stable she'd experienced in a while came over her.

"We would, that's who. I can get us to Huddig. Can you remember how to get us to the cabin?"

Holly closed her eyes and called up some of her deepest memories. She'd learned long ago that remembering good times with Brody reopened wounds, made her desolate and lonely and tempted her to blame herself for the failures of the marriage. If only she'd been more responsive. If only she'd nagged him less often. If only she'd put Brody first, before Georgia.

If only, if only, if only.

But, right now, letting snapshots of moments at the cabin flood in on her, all she felt was determination to rescue her daughter.

"Yes," she said, opening her eyes again. "I know how to get there."

"Then let's go."

"Let's go." She settled her shoulders into her seat as he pushed the car even further to its limits. "Let's get Georgia back."

NINE

They weren't at Taco Tim's.

Taco Tim's wasn't even open. From the look of things, it had been closed for some time.

Holly silently cried as Ryan drove through the empty gravel parking lot. His headlights swept over a group of teenagers draped across the lone picnic table. They looked offended at having their fun interrupted.

"I should have known," Holly said, wiping her nose with a napkin that Ryan had found for her in his glove box. It was the least he could do. He hated this feeling of helplessness. "It's too late. Nobody's eating tacos at a roadside stand in the middle of nowhere at nine o'clock at night."

"Are you sure it's this one?"

"Absolutely sure." She paused, wiped again, took a deep, watery breath. "Do you think this means Georgia's hungry?"

"No," he said without even thinking about it, wanting to erase whatever worries he could from Holly's mind, if worries could be erased. "I'm sure he stopped and got her something else."

Her hands twitched around her phone, and Ryan knew that she wanted to try calling again. But she'd already tried so many times, and her call had gotten bumped to voicemail every time. Brody had most certainly shut off the phone. He wanted to be in charge of the communication between them. It was a power play.

He also probably was worried that they may somehow trace his whereabouts if he kept the phone line open. And maybe they would have, if Holly had allowed the police to be involved in their search.

"You know, we should really give the Huddig PD a heads-up," he suggested softly.

"No," she said, just as quickly as he'd said it a moment ago. "He said no police."

"But if something should go wrong…"

"What do you mean? I thought you said we couldn't think that way."

Ryan didn't respond. He wasn't sure how to, without setting off more worries for her. But he didn't need to say anything for her to know exactly what he was thinking.

"I see," she said. "You're worried that he will kill me."

"I'm not going to let that happen."

"If you can stop it. But there's a part of you that's worried you won't be able to."

No, Ryan thought. He'll have to kill me first. Because that's the only possible way I'm going to let him get to you.

But he couldn't voice that out loud, because the last thing Holly needed was him inserting a worry she hadn't thought of yet.

She turned back toward the window. "Sometimes I think he started killing me a long time ago and is just now getting around to finishing the job."

"He won't. Not if I have anything to say about it."

She kept her face toward the window, but Ryan could see her reflection. She gave a thin smile. "Ryan Oldham, ever the hero."

"Not a hero. Just a friend who cares."

A slight nod. "A friend who cares." If Ryan wasn't mistaken, there was some bitterness lacing the edges of the word *friend* when she said it. This was a sore subject that they didn't need to dance around again. Not right now.

"Can you think of anyplace else to look for on the way? Anyplace Brody always stops at on his way down to the cabin?"

"Not until you get down there. He usually would stop at a tackle shop for some bait, but that's about it. We would go to the store once we got settled. But it's late. That store won't be open. Neither will the tackle shop."

Ryan glanced at the clock. They still had hours to go. He was awake, on alert, ready. But Holly looked tired. The worry and adrenaline had worn on her. Not to mention she'd only just reached town that afternoon. She'd already come from a long drive.

And he had no idea what the adrenaline had done to Brody. Was he a live wire waiting to be crossed? Or was he fighting fatigue, his eyelids feeling heavy, his brain ready to check out?

Once again, Holly seemed to read his mind.

"We're going to have to stop soon," she said. "I don't want to pass him because we can't see him in the dark."

"Okay," Ryan said. "We'll look for someplace to stay."

Holly hated the way she felt. Powerless. Vulnerable. Defeated.

She was fuzzy, as if she were trying to see through a bedsheet. It was more than 1,500 miles from Los Angeles to Garnett. She'd broken it up as best she could, but even their last overnight in Liberal was nearly six hours away from their destination. It seemed like a lifetime ago that she'd driven it, but it was only that morning. She was exhausted.

Nothing was clear to her anymore. Her thoughts were drained, her eyes were strained, her brain was tired. She could easily walk right past Brody and not even realize it.

But not Georgia, she thought. I would never walk right past Georgia.

But could she drive past? Especially since she wasn't even the one doing the driving?

They had to stop. She didn't want to miss something in the dark. Get down to Huddig, only to realize that Brody had taken their daughter somewhere else. And then they'd be eight hours down the road, if not more. They would never catch her.

And then what? You're not going to suddenly come up with five million.

You'll lose her either way.

No, they had to stop. It felt wrong and counter to the search, but she knew it needed to be done.

"There's a Snooze Inn." She pointed up ahead. "That should work."

Ryan nodded and flicked on his turn signal, aiming for the off-ramp to take them to the hotel.

It felt like surrender, leaving the highway. She wasn't ready to surrender to Brody Shipley. She would never be ready to surrender.

But had she surrendered when it came to Ryan? She thought maybe she had. She watched him as he navigated the parking lot, his focus sharp and determined. He would go on for a thousand more hours, a million more miles, if that was what it took. She knew this without him saying a word. Because that was who Ryan was. Generous and fearless. Handsome and kind.

And still out of her reach.

Brody used to tell her, after beating her, that he deserved better than her. That he deserved someone with the guts to stand up for herself. It baffled her that he didn't see she shouldn't have to have guts to stand up for herself against the man who supposedly loved her. But that didn't seem to matter. What mattered was that somewhere along the line, she started to believe him.

It had taken guts to forge ahead with the life of a single mom. She hadn't taken that role by choice, but she lived it, embraced it, grew into it. She saw how wrong Brody was about her. She deserved better than him.

Every time she thought about that, images of Ryan's smile popped unbidden into her mind. And every time, she swept them away.

It was too late for her and Ryan. If they never were

together before all these complications, they sure weren't going to be now.

Funny how in the middle of all her fatigued murkiness, this was the one thing that had become clear to her.

Ryan pulled into a parking spot.

"I'll check us in," he said, "if you want to stay here."

Holly nodded. Now that she was this close to crashing for the night, the adrenaline had receded, and the thought of so much as moving a leg to stand was too complicated of a task for her to handle.

He got out and shut the door. The silence in the car pressed in on her. She began to sing the Pedigreen Soup jingle under her breath. And then louder. And louder still, tears running down her face as she stroked Georgia's stuffed kitty and stared at her phone, willing it to ring.

At the very least, a check-in from Lynne would have been nice.

She opened her text messages. Still nothing.

It was true she'd developed a suspicion that God had listened to and answered her one big prayer—*Please help me find the strength and the money to raise this little girl alone*—and then hung up the phone. But she was desperate, and any time she was desperate, she turned to the one source of comfort she'd come to rely on the most. Her bedtime prayers would be long and impassioned tonight. Surely God wouldn't ignore her now, in her time of need.

She held the kitty up and stared into its little gold eyes. Its whiskers were bent and crumpled from years of love. "Who will you sleep with tonight, Kitty?" She pressed the stuffed animal to her chest and let her head fall back against the headrest, realizing that this would be the first time in all of Georgia's life that she will have not kissed her goodnight. "Don't worry, Georgia. Kitty can sleep with me. I'll keep her safe. You just stay safe…wherever you are."

But the image of Georgia trying to fall asleep without her favorite stuffed toy was more than Holly could take.

She redialed Brody's number and put the phone on speaker.

He didn't answer. Of course he didn't. She was dumped into his voicemail. The sound of his recorded voice made her skin crawl, but she waited for the beep anyway.

"Brody. Georgia needs her kitten. She always sleeps with it. Always. I have it. Please tell me where you are. Please."

But there was only silence on the other end, and eventually she simply hung up.

Ryan wasn't supposed to be a police officer right now. He was supposed to be a friend, but that was impossible. When you had protect-and-serve blood coursing through your veins, you never truly turned it off. He was on edge as he crossed the parking lot into the hotel lobby but only due to his usual vigilance. That he felt the need to have eyes in every direction at once.

He didn't like leaving Holly alone in the parking lot. When he'd shut the car door, he'd tapped the window to remind her to lock it. But she was studying the stuffed toy they'd found in Brody's car so intently that she hadn't heard him. And he hadn't had the heart to tap again to interrupt her. He would just remain watchful.

Because that's what cops do.

He came in through the lobby door backward, getting one last look at the car and the parking lot before turning around.

"Can I help you?" the clerk asked.

"Hi. Yeah. I need two rooms. Preferably next to each other. Hoping you have availability?"

"Sure do."

"Can you put us on the front side of the hotel?" He gestured toward the parking lot. He wanted to be able to see the highway from his window. Just in case he couldn't sleep.

"Absolutely." The clerk took Ryan's credit card, tapped around on the computer, then grabbed a couple of key-cards and pushed them across the counter. She pointed out the door. "Right up front here."

"Thank you."

"Anything else you need?"

No. He just needed to get Holly safely inside. He needed to get some rest. He needed… His stomach growled.

"Got any food around here?"

She nodded toward the door again. "Take a left like you're going to the pool. We've got a couple of vending machines there. Stay away from the peanuts. They've been in there forever. Probably break your teeth. Nobody ever buys the peanuts."

"Thank you," he said, taking the cards.

He took a mental inventory of the cars in the lot as he walked back to the car. Ironically, there were not one, but two, white sedans.

If only it had been that easy when we were looking for one earlier, he thought.

A handful of semis idled at the edges of the lot, and a beat-up Jeep was parked outside the farthest room. Not a single blue truck to be found. He considered the real possibility that Brody had switched cars once again, or that their deduction about the cabin was wrong and he was headed in the opposite direction—two scenarios that Ryan didn't even want to think about. How would Holly react to arriving at the cabin and finding it empty? They would be so far from home.

Holly was holding the stuffed cat to her chest, still gazing out to nowhere while she stroked its head with her thumb. He knocked on her window and held up the keycards.

"You hungry?" he asked. "There's a machine."

She shook her head. "I'm too tired to be hungry. Too worried."

Holly got out and they made their way to their rooms. He handed her a keycard and she stood at her door with it, looking lost and small and sad.

"Just…let me know if you need anything, then? You can call or…you can knock on the wall. I'll hear you."

Holly nodded, then slowly opened her room door, still clutching the beat-up stuffed cat in one hand. "Good night," she said. "And, Ryan, thank you. For everything. Truly."

"Of course."

There was a slight hesitation, during which Ryan was sure she wanted to say something, before she nodded and disappeared inside. He heard the dead bolt turn and watched as she swiftly shut the curtains.

"Good night," he said, softly, to himself, and then let himself into his room.

It was dank and musty inside, and the overhead light flickered purplish-blue against the orange-painted walls and the orange-and-brown floral curtains. The garish and ugly decor came straight out of a decade long since passed, but when he sank onto the bed, he didn't care what it looked like.

Holly must feel just as spent. He stretched his legs out across the bed and leaned back against the wall, wondering if Holly was leaning against the wall on her side, only a couple thin sheets of wallboard separating their shoulders. He closed his eyes and imagined them back-to-back, eyes closed, breath slowing, in tune with each other. The image warmed and comforted him.

I have to stop thinking like this. She's not mine. She never will be.

It was never meant to be for them, and the sooner Ryan accepted that fact, the sooner he could move on with his life, as he should have done years ago.

His phone buzzed, startling him. He snatched it out of his pocket, thinking maybe it was Holly. That something was wrong and she needed him.

It was his older sister, Savannah. He breathed a sigh of relief and brought the phone to his ear.

"Hey, Savannah."

"Where are you?"

"Why?"

"I made a huge pan of lasagna, and David and I can't eat it all, so I brought you some. But you're not home. Obviously."

"Just use your key," he said.

"Already did," she said. "But that doesn't answer my question. Where are you? I thought maybe I'd see you at the fair tonight. You have a hot date or something?" Ryan heard the telltale sound of his refrigerator opening and closing, then the sounds of water running and glassware clinking.

"Are you doing the dishes? You don't need to be doing my dishes."

"You're avoiding the question. Which must mean you're on a hot date. Is Morgan in town? Do I need to let you go?"

"Seriously, Savannah, I'm capable of doing the dishes."

"Relax. I'm lollygagging so David has to handle the kids' bath and bedtime by himself. Dishes are light work." She giggled. "So…?"

"So…" Ryan was used to telling Savannah everything about his life, but he wasn't sure what he could or should divulge about his current situation. "I'm helping a friend. She's in a bad situation. I might not be home for a couple of days."

The water turned off. "That sounds serious."

"It is serious."

"Are you safe? Who's the friend?"

"We are both safe right now. And it's…" He paused,

trying to remember what Savannah's relationship with Holly was. He vaguely recalled sitting on Savannah's bed nursing his wounds after Holly left, while Savannah played breakup songs on her stereo and talked about fish and the sea. "It's Holly."

Now there was a pause on Savannah's end, the only sounds the underwater bumping around of dishes. "Holly Hampton?" she finally asked incredulously.

"It's Shipley now, remember?"

"Oh, that's right. She ran off with Brody Shipley after high school. I remember." She chuckled. "I haven't thought about that guy in ages. She still with him?"

"No," Ryan said darkly.

"Ah. So she's having relationship problems and you're coming to her rescue. Very high school. How noble of you, Ryan."

"That's putting it mildly, but yes, something like that," Ryan said. "And I'm helping her, not coming to her rescue. She doesn't need a knight in shining armor."

"If I remember correctly, you held quite a torch for that girl. And she broke your heart. You were crushed when she left. Why are you getting wrapped up with her again?"

"I'm not. I'm just helping a friend. Can we let it drop now?"

The water turned on and Savannah chuckled again. "Sure. Okay. By the way, you missed some big drama at the fair. I heard that some kid got snatched. Threw the whole fair into a tizzy. A kidnapping right here in Garnett—can you believe it? It's supposedly all over the internet because the kid looked just like that little girl in the *Precipitators* movie. Waterfall?"

"Icefall," he corrected. "And I know. I was there."

"Oh," Savannah said, and then, "Ooohhh. Are you sure you're safe?"

"As safe as I can be," he said.

"Okay. Stay safe." He heard the gurgle of the sink plug being pulled. "Well, I'm going to finish up here and then I'll go. I'll tell Mom you're still alive and the house is still standing. There's garlic bread in the fridge, too, by the way. Good stuff."

"Thanks, Savannah."

"Anytime, little bro. And Ry?"

"Yeah?"

"Don't just protect her. Protect yourself, too, okay?"

"I'm safe. I'm trained for this stuff, remember?"

"I meant your heart, Ry. Protect that."

He'd heard that from Savannah before. On more than one occasion, the most recent being when he was wrestling with the Morgan decision. Savannah cared. She just wanted him to be happy, and he was lucky to have her.

"I will. I mean, I already am."

"Uh-huh. Maybe pray on it for a minute. You could probably use some outside support. Or is it inside support when it's God?"

He chuckled. "Probably. Bye."

"Bye!"

He tossed the phone to the side, letting it bounce across the mattress. He knew that his sister was right. He was so busy protecting, he wasn't nearly as protected as he needed to be. He was telling himself that he was over Holly Shipley, that he was just helping out as a friend and that he was letting her go, but he wasn't sure if his heart had gotten the message.

Maybe he did need some inside help.

He let his head flop forward and clasped his hands in front of him. He wasn't sure what to pray for. He believed that Holly was right on some level—*be careful what you ask for in life, because you just might get it.*

In the end, he prayed for resilience. Because, when it came to Holly, that was the protection he needed most of all.

After he finished his prayer, he rested his head back against the wall again and closed his eyes.

He didn't even realize he'd fallen asleep until he woke with a start, sunlight streaming through the crack between his curtains.

And the sound of commotion right outside his door.

TEN

It was the sound of the Pedigreen song that ripped Holly awake. In her dream, she was running through the hay maze again, calling Georgia's name. The confusion and dread was as palpable as it had been in real life. She could almost smell the hay, could almost feel it scratching her arms as she rushed through the maze.

But then in her dream, she heard Georgia's voice, singing that silly soup commercial song. Getting it wrong in all the same places. Stopping to giggle at her own mispronunciation and starting again. But the voice was muffled, far away. Just around the next corner...and the next...and the next...

And then Brody's impatient voice, loud and clear, telling her to stop with that incessant singing and get a move on, they've already lost enough time.

That was the part that pulled Holly out of her dream.

"Georgia?" she asked, sitting upright on her bed. It took her a minute to remember where she was or why she was there. She barely registered the strip of sunlight that was coming through the curtains before she heard the voice again.

"Just get in the truck. We've got to go."

"But my kitty."

"Would you stop about the kitty? I'll get you a new toy. Your mom spoiled you. Get in."

Holly was off the bed and across the room, hand outstretched to grasp the doorknob, before she even fully realized that she was moving. She ripped the door open and sucked in a breath, unable to believe what she was seeing. Afraid that she was still dreaming.

Georgia stood just feet away, right outside Ryan's door, facing the sidewalk, thumb in her mouth. Georgia rarely sucked her thumb anymore; her acting coach made sure of it. She only did it when she was tired or feeling uneasy. She glanced at Holly, popped her thumb out of her mouth and lit up at the same time that Holly lunged for her.

"Mommy!"

"Georgia! Baby!"

She scooped up her daughter and wrapped her into a tight hug, hardly believing that what she was feeling was real. She had the briefest thought that, if this was part of her dream, she didn't want to wake up.

"Mommy, you're squeezing," Georgia said into her neck.

But Holly had come back to reality and caught Brody's eye. He stood at the hood of his truck, fumbling in his jeans pocket for keys, his mouth drawn into a grimace, teeth showing. He leaned forward, ready to launch. Holly understood immediately what he intended to do.

"In the truck, Georgia," he growled.

Holly had spent so much of her life afraid of this man. Physically cowering from him. Begging him not to hurt her.

But at this moment, she felt powerful against him, the kind of power that came from knowing she would fight and lose everything if she had to, just to keep from losing this one thing.

She clutched Georgia tighter. The child, seeming to understand at last that things were not okay, grunted, but didn't protest against her mother's tight grip. Holly wanted to get Georgia inside, where she was safe, but she also knew that the moment she was no longer holding the child, she would be Brody's fair game.

She was also a good ten feet from the open front door of her room.

But only inches away from Ryan's door.

She was finally able to make her hand pull away from Georgia's back. She reached behind her blindly, refusing to break eye contact with Brody. She pawed air and shuffled backward until she found Ryan's door, then pounded with the flat of her palm.

"Ryan," she said, surprised at how calm she sounded. Very different from how she felt inside.

"That is a bad idea," Brody said. He had dropped into a slow, quiet voice that Holly recognized, and it chilled her to the bone.

"Ryan!"

"Put her down, Holly. You don't want this fight."

"There's no fight," she answered, her voice ragged and tight. "She's staying here. With me. And you're going to jail. You can't just…take her, Brody."

"She's my daughter."

"She doesn't even know you."

Georgia pulled her thumb out of her mouth. "That's Daddy," she said. But she sounded uncertain, as if she knew something was wrong but couldn't quite comprehend what it was. Holly was heartened to know that at least Georgia hadn't been traumatized.

"She's my daughter," Brody repeated, stepping up onto the curb to approach them. "Say goodbye, Holly. I warned you, but you never have listened to me. And now you're going to see how serious I am." He faked a lunge at Holly.

She refused to flinch. Not anymore.

Ryan whipped open the door. He rushed past Holly in a blur, and she hurriedly backed into his room, nearly stumbling over the threshold. Safely inside, Holly let the door slam shut, enveloping them in dark shadows. Georgia whimpered and Holly's heart hurt. She knew it was unrealistic to expect even someone as sweet and sunny as Georgia to get kidnapped and be unfazed by it.

She just hated that the part that made her whine was their reunion.

She kissed the top of Georgia's head, breathing in her scent, closing her eyes to try and convince herself that this was real and she was holding her daughter again, and she was okay. She gave her a quick once-over to be sure.

Thank You, God. Thank You, thank You.

"What's going on?" Georgia asked, ever the inquisitive one. "Why is Daddy…why are you crying? Mommy.

I lost Kitty, Mommy." And this was at last the thing
that broke Georgia. That she lost her stuffed cat. The
one thing that Holly could fix. Georgia started to cry.

"I have it," Holly said. "Don't worry. I have Kitty.
She's in my room next door."

"I want her," Georgia cried, sounding for the first
time in just about as long as Holly could remember like
a five-year-old on the edge of a tantrum instead of a
resigned adult.

"I'll get her for you soon," she said. "I promise."

She could hear muffled voices outside the door, es-
calating. If Ryan was expecting Brody to put up his
hands and surrender, he was going to be disappointed.
Brody was not the surrendering type. He wasn't about
to start now.

Georgia wriggled and squirmed, trying to extricate
herself. "Can I watch TV?"

Holly's heart panged. Georgia was okay. Maybe she
wasn't too traumatized. All Holly had to do was play
along. Everything was normal.

Nothing to see here; certainly not a kidnapping, no.

She gave Georgia one last squeeze, then set her down.
"Sure. Of course."

Georgia scampered to the TV stand and snatched up
the remote, then sat on the edge of the bed, her brow
wrinkled with concentration as she pushed buttons.

Holly edged toward the window, where she could
see through the crack in the slightly parted curtains.
She held her breath. The truth was, she had no idea
where this went from here. She'd only focused on getting Georgia back, but she'd never even considered

what might happen next. She supposed she had a vague image of Brody behind bars, but there were so many steps between rescuing Georgia and putting away Brody that she couldn't quite wrap her mind around what they were.

But she looked out just in time to see Brody dive into his truck and back out of the parking space. Without missing a beat, Ryan raced to his own car and jumped in.

The muffled yelling ended in the squealing of tires and hail of loose gravel as two vehicles screeched out of the parking lot.

Brody had promised bad things if Holly so much as even considered calling the police. She'd held off for as long as she could. But she had Georgia back, and she couldn't sit by and wait any longer. This was Ryan's life on the line. Who knew where Brody would lead him, and if the chase ended in a trap, Ryan was going to need backup.

Holly lunged across the bed and dialed 9-1-1. She tried to keep her voice calm for Georgia, even though on the inside she was raging with alarm.

"9-1-1. What's your emergency?"

"Hello? Um, my name is Holly Shipley. My ex-husband, um…took my daughter. I've got her back now, but my friend is chasing him on the highway. He's a Garnett PD officer. I'm afraid he could be in trouble. He's going to need help…"

For the next ten minutes, Holly described Brody's truck, Ryan's car and their exact location. She recounted, cryptically, what had happened. Somehow, she was cold and sweating at the same time.

By the time she hung up, Holly was breathless, left only with the musical voices of cartoon characters and a hope that Ryan would come back to her alive.

There was no time to think, only time to react. *Key in ignition, foot on pedal, eyes on mirrors, follow the blue truck. Vigilance, vigilance, vigilance.*

Ryan was aware of rocks kicking up and pinging the sides of his car, of gravel from Brody's tires flinging all the way to his windshield, of clouds of dust and exhaust left in their wake. He was aware of cars swerving to the side of the road and drivers in various states of alarm and irritation as they whizzed by.

But he was really only focused on staying with Brody.

He had no plan for what happened after that. He had his gun, but nothing else. No handcuffs or pepper spray. No baton. No radio.

And, worse than that, he had no real idea what weapons Brody might have on him. He could be driving into a fight he couldn't win.

He'd gone against his instincts because Holly had begged him to, and because Brody had made a promise of danger if she didn't comply with his wishes. She was scared, but he knew she would do it alone if he insisted on throwing police tactics at the problem. The idea of something happening to her was more than Ryan could bear. He'd come to her aid with nothing but a sidearm and a determination that he would be successful in returning her daughter to her.

Georgia was back in her arms, but that wasn't enough. Holly was safe for now. But if Ryan didn't catch Brody, she would never feel safe knowing he was out there somewhere.

She'll hide, and I'll lose her again.

I would've had to have her in order to lose her.

Brody led Ryan right back to the highway, nearly plowing through a minivan to get down the ramp. Ryan gripped the steering wheel hard, the nose of his car only inches from Brody's back bumper. The minivan honked as he sped past, but he couldn't let that distract him. They hit the highway at nearly 100 miles an hour, leaving bewildered, honking drivers in their wake.

Brody darted through traffic as if he'd been the subject of a million police chases. Ryan, who'd never yet pursued a suspect who didn't immediately comply, gritted his teeth and followed, sweat lining his forehead and the back of his neck.

Please, God, don't let us cause any wrecks today.

He cut too close to a Cadillac, and the Caddy veered, then lost control and fishtailed, leaving a cloud of dust as it came to a stop against a guardrail. The Cadillac let out a long honk, reminding Ryan that he was in his own car, not a police cruiser, so as far as that driver knew, he was just playing around. He glanced in the rearview and could see the driver of the Cadillac standing outside the car, a phone pressed to his ear as he stared down the highway at the speeding cars. It hadn't even dawned on Ryan that a driver might call the police and take that decision out of his hands. The problem was, the police would have no way of knowing that Ryan was one of them. He needed to stop Brody before they mobilized.

Ryan returned his eyes to the road just in time to see Brody dart onto an off-ramp, again forcing cars to screech to a stop on the side of the road. If they didn't slow down, someone was going to get hurt.

But if he did slow down and Brody got away, it was Holly who would get hurt.

He was so close to putting this thing to an end. So close.

Brody didn't turn at the top of the ramp. Instead, he bolted through cross-traffic and down the ramp on the other side, right back onto the highway. A car skidded to a stop to miss him, the car behind that one not as quick on the brakes. It slammed into the stopped car with just enough force to jar that car right into Ryan's path. He jerked the wheel to the side at the last minute, his left front fender barely clipping the right front fender of the other car.

He knew he should stop. He knew he should make sure the other driver was okay.

But he couldn't stop. Brody had already gained ground.

God, forgive me, and help that person.

Ryan gunned it and plunged down the opposite ramp and back onto the highway behind Brody. The bump with the other car had cost him. He was going to have to really push it if he wanted to keep up. He heard Holly's voice in his head, urging him not to give up, and pressed harder on the gas, ignoring the new rattle coming from the front of the car, the new tug on the steering wheel to the left.

"Come on, come on," he said, leaning forward.

The next time Brody took a ramp, Ryan was prepared to cross traffic again. He laid on his horn just to let people know they were coming. At the last possible second, though, Brody turned. Ryan was still lagging behind, but there was no cross-traffic to contend with so he was able to see the back end of Brody's truck as he turned again onto a gravel back road, surrounded by high fields of corn, throwing up a cloud of dust.

Brody wasn't stupid—Ryan would give him that. From a distance, or from the sky, the dust would give him away immediately. But luring Ryan into a chase inside the cloud of dust stripped away Ryan's orientation and limited his visibility. He was following blindly, hoping he was getting closer but having no real idea. He pushed harder and harder, faster and faster, his tires slipping over rock, corn stalks slapping the sides of his car, twice missing turns until he was past them, unsure whether Brody took them or not, skidding to a stop, throwing his car into reverse and taking the chance.

It wasn't until he was completely out of the dust, his vision clear, that he realized Brody had lost him. They were deep in cornfields now. Brody must have found a turnoff somewhere, or Ryan must have guessed incorrectly and turned off when Brody didn't. Even if he turned around, retraced where he'd been, Ryan knew that if he were to find the truck, there would be no one in it. Ryan eased up on the gas, his car slowing. He came to a stop and peered in the rearview mirror. Dust floated everywhere. If Brody had left his truck and run into the corn, he would be even harder to find. Maybe impossible.

Ryan struck the steering wheel with his fist.

Brody had gotten away.

Which meant Brody Shipley, a man dangerous enough to kidnap his daughter at a public fair and threaten to murder his ex if he didn't get what he wanted, was at large.

And Holly was far from out of danger.

ELEVEN

"And then we eated hamburgers in the truck," Georgia said, rattling off every detail of her adventure with Brody. "And I felt sick after and he was mad because he said we were running behind but we had to stop so I wouldn't frow up in his car."

Of course. Brody didn't know that Georgia got carsick when she was tired. Holly had mopped up more accidents than she could count in the back seat of her own car.

Holly had to be grateful on some level that Brody had been so absent in Georgia's life. It was his ignorance that forced them to stop at the same hotel. Had they not, and had she not been awakened by Georgia's singing, they might have missed each other. This day would have started the way the last one ended.

She hadn't heard from Ryan since he left. She'd briefly talked to a police officer on the sidewalk outside Ryan's room, describing the vehicles and explaining the situation, and then listened to the sirens swell and fade. After the sirens had disappeared altogether, the room was filled with eerie silence, save for Georgia's running dialogue. Holly couldn't let her mind wander, to go down a path of what-if. She'd only just reconnected with Ryan. The thought of something happening to him because of her was more than she could take in at the moment.

He's smart, Holly. He's experienced. He knows what he's doing and he knows how to handle someone like Brody.

Yes, but she hadn't let him leave prepared. She'd tied his hands. She was the one who put him in danger.

"But I didn't get sick."

Holly reached down and stroked Georgia's hair, in part to take her mind off Ryan, and in part just to make sure that her daughter really was there and not a figment of her imagination.

"I'm glad you didn't get sick," she said. "And I'm glad you stopped here. I missed you."

"I missed you, too, Mommy," Georgia said, before rattling on. "And then the lady at the front desk said I looked familiar and Daddy told her to mind her own business and made me wait in the truck until we had a room. And I told him that you don't like it when people recognize me, either, and he said you shoulda thought of that before you let me be in a movie because you can't put toothpaste back in the tube." She covered her mouth and giggled. "Isn't that funny, Mommy? Putting toothpaste back in a tube?"

"Uh-huh," Holly said, trying not to go down a path of woulda-shoulda-coulda. And trying not to think about the things Brody should've thought about before acting, too. Like abandoning his wife and daughter without so much as a goodbye. Like stealing his daughter and trying to extort money out of Holly.

He was probably thinking of some shouldas for himself right now, with Ryan on his tail.

She glanced at her phone, and her thoughts about Ryan began to spiral again. She had to remind herself that, while Brody was desperate, he was smart enough to know that even in desperation, he shouldn't mess with Ryan. Ryan was bigger and leaner and much more muscular than Brody.

But, then again, Brody was desperate, and he had to know that Holly wouldn't just take Georgia back and forget anything ever happened. He knew that he would be on the run for the rest of his life.

As if on cue, her phone rang.

"Finally." She picked it up, fully expecting Ryan. But instead, Brody's number popped up on the screen. She dropped the phone on the bed as if it were on fire and pressed her hand to her mouth, barely stifling a gasp.

"What, Mommy?" Georgia asked, glancing back at her. "Your phone?"

Holly swallowed to steady herself. "It's all good, baby," she said, and thumbed the phone to silent. She couldn't do it. She couldn't talk to Brody if it meant she would hear the worst.

Oh, Ryan. What's happened to you?

Guilt coursed through her body. He'd risked it all because she'd asked him to. And for what? A relationship that never was and never would be?

Her heart ached in her chest. Their relationship never

was, and that was because of her, too. And it never would be, because she didn't see how it was possible.

Georgia couldn't live the normal life of a five-year-old because Holly had asked God to help her set up Georgia to have a life different from hers. Georgia was here in Garnett because Holly needed to think. Georgia was snatched away because Holly was busy rekindling an old flame that would never turn into a fire.

All of it—*every single thing*—was Holly's fault.

Maybe that was it. It wasn't *Be careful what you pray for, because you might get it*. It was Holly praying for the wrong thing. She should have been praying for the strength and wisdom to take care of herself.

Tears welled on her bottom lids.

"What, Mommy?" Georgia asked again, this time standing and putting her tiny, warm hands on each of Holly's cheeks—something she often did when Holly was upset. Even this was too much for Holly to stand. The simplest gesture from her kind, sweet daughter.

Tears spilled over. Holly quickly brushed them away, grabbed Georgia's wrists and kissed each of her little palms. "Nothing, sweetie. I'm just so glad you had such a fun adventure is all."

Georgia looked skeptical. She was little, but she was wise. And she knew her mother. She used one tiny pointer finger to trace each tear down Holly's cheeks, smudging them into her skin until they were gone. She frowned, bent to pick up Kitty, which Holly had crept back to her room to retrieve, and turned back to the TV.

"Daddy doesn't like cartoons."

The phone stopped buzzing. Holly stared at it. She

felt like some sort of lifeline between Ryan and her was gone, even though she knew Brody was anything but a lifeline. Quite the opposite, actually. Maybe they were still in the chase. Maybe Brody was calling to tell her to make Ryan back off.

She picked up the phone and stared at it, contemplating whether to call Brody back.

"Right, Mommy?"

"Huh?"

"I said you like cartoons though, right?"

"Oh. Uh-huh. Sure, baby."

"I like cartoons, too. And so does Kitty. Right, Kitty?"

She wouldn't call Brody back. She wouldn't give him the satisfaction. If Ryan were hurt, Brody would hardly tell her where to send help. Holly chewed her lip and listened to Georgia prattle on. Every few minutes, she glanced down at the phone in her hand, her heart growing more and more worried with each passing second.

After what seemed like an impossible amount of time, a knock sounded at the door, and Georgia's voice faded away. Holly went cold. Ryan wouldn't knock on his own door, would he? He would have at the very least called her, right?

Brody. Of course it was Brody. He'd tried calling and she didn't answer, so he would show up at her doorstep. She had been foolish to stay at the hotel. She didn't breathe, didn't move. The knock came again, and she had to press her lips together to keep from crying out. She would try to convince him that she was gone, but surely he could hear the TV through the door. Surely he could hear Georgia's voice.

Georgia glanced at the door. "There's someone here," she said, as if Holly hadn't heard the knock herself.

"It's probably no one," Holly said, trying to sound uninterested. "Oh, he drank a potion and turned purple!" She pointed at the TV screen. Once upon a time, she'd sworn she would never introduce Georgia to television, would raise her to entertain herself. If someone had told her back then that she would be using the TV to distract Georgia from a knocking on a hotel room door that could be coming from her murderous, kidnapping father, she would have never believed it.

But then again, there were a lot of things about her life that she wouldn't have believed back then.

Georgia let out a giggle, and Holly nearly jumped out of her skin.

"Funny, Mommy. Did you see that? Now he's green." She was pointing at the TV, oblivious to what was about to go down. Holly's tactic had worked.

The knock returned, and she jumped again. He knew she was in here.

How long would she have before he broke the door down to get to her?

How long could she fight to stay alive in front of her daughter?

Because make no mistake about it.

Now that Brody had gotten Ryan, he was here to kill her.

In his haste to follow Brody, Ryan had left the key-card to his room on the nightstand. But from the sound of cartoon television voices through the door, Holly was still inside, which would save him a trip to the office for a replacement key.

But it also meant he would have to face Holly right away.

Face her with his failure.

He'd spent the last hour driving through cornfields and mazes of adjacent back roads, listening as police sirens grew closer and then faded out again. He wasn't the one who'd gotten the police involved—probably witnesses called it in or maybe the man whom he'd hit-and-run—but now that they were, he needed to contact the department with an update.

Heavier on his mind was the fact that he would need to break the news to Holly: Brody was gone. He'd lost him. And he would have to face up to that. Not only was Brody still loose, but the police involvement meant that now she was in even more danger. She'd been dead set against getting the police involved, but now it was out of their hands.

He took a deep breath and knocked, softly at first, but when there was no answer, he tried again, a little harder.

"Holly? Are you in there? It's me."

He raised his fist to knock again, but, thankfully, the door whipped open. Holly's startled face peered out at him.

"Ryan?" She let out a breath and threw the door open, flinging herself around his neck with such force that he barely had time to brace himself to keep from getting tackled to the ground. "Oh, thank goodness you're okay. I thought… I thought…" She pulled away, shook her head as if to chase away the rest of the sentence and swallowed. "Are you okay ? What happened?"

Ryan lowered his head. Now that he was here, he was unable to find the words.

She held up her phone. "I know he said not to, but… I couldn't stand the thought of you being out there with no backup."

"You're the one who called the police?"

She nodded. "But also, he's been calling me. I haven't answered. What happened?"

He forced himself to look her in the eye. "He got away. Lost me on some gravel roads in a cornfield. I got behind when someone hit me, and—"

Holly tensed, interrupting him. "You got hit? Are you okay?"

"I'm fine. Car's a little dinged up is all. Just cost me time."

Not true, he thought. Time wasn't the only thing it cost you. It also cost you the chase. It may have cost you Holly's life.

But that was a reality he wasn't ready to face yet. Now that this had happened, he was determined to put everything on the line to keep her secure. Even more than he already had. "I'm so sorry, Holly. I'll find him. I promise."

The reality of what he was saying must have set in, because Holly seemed to grow smaller and smaller next to him, her phone clutched hard in her fist. She backed up and dropped on the edge of the bed, lost in concentration. He couldn't tell if she was quaking from fear or from mustering up resolve.

"No," she said, firmly enough that Georgia looked up from the TV, glanced at Holly and then at Ryan before going back to watching.

She's much more intuitive than we realize, Ryan thought. She knows that something is not right, but she also knows now is not the time to check things out for herself. She trusts her mother. I trust her, too. I just hope she hasn't lost trust in me.

"No," Holly repeated. "You're not the one who needs to apologize. You've done nothing but help. You've gone out of your way, put yourself in danger, wrecked your car and all for what? For…" She trailed off, and Ryan guessed that was because she could see the answer in his eyes. "For me," she finished quietly.

"I did it because I…"

I've never forgotten you and don't want to lose you again.

"Because I took an oath to serve and protect."

"Right," she said, and he could swear she was building armor around herself using just that one word. *Rightrightrightrightright…* She took a deep breath and lifted her chin. "Well, now that we have Georgia, we can go home. And you can return to—well, I guess to normal life."

"What will you do?"

"I don't know. Make a police report and pray they find him before he finds me? Maybe go back to California. Maybe stay. Hope that Brody forgets?"

Her phone buzzed and she lifted it, gave a wan smile and turned it toward him so that he was looking at Brody's number. "So much for that last thought, huh?" She thumbed the call away. "He'll never forget, as long as he lives. We'll leave for California right away and pray he doesn't follow us."

"If you stay, I'll protect you."

"That's the problem," she said. "We'll be a burden to you. You don't need that burden. It's easier to hide in California."

"It's not impossible for him to find you there."

"I know, but it's the best I've got."

"You've got me."

"Ryan."

If you go, he wanted to say, when will I ever see you again?

Maybe that was part of why she'd made the decision. She didn't want to see him again. She wanted to go away.

Her phone buzzed again. She stared at it. "One thing's for certain. We can't stay here. He knows where we are. We've got to move before he comes back."

For whatever reason, she couldn't bring herself to block the number, even though Brody was calling her nonstop, a constant, humming stress that would surely drive her crazy if she let it go on much longer. She denied the call and then two minutes later would have to deny it again.

Maybe this will just become part of my life. Brody always in my back pocket, nagging at me.

Until he's in your face.

Or until he finds you, and then there's no more you to nag at.

But something about having him in her consciousness comforted her. If he were in her back pocket, that meant he wasn't waiting for her just around the corner. It meant he wasn't bearing down on her from across the room, ready to unleash his fury. He was the voice on the other end of the phone, not the shadow in the parking lot.

She and Ryan were going to meet at his car in five minutes to go home. There was nothing to pack, really, but she went back over to her room to grab her overnight bag that she hadn't even opened.

"Mommy? Are we going back to Nana Cheryl's house?" Georgia stood just inside the doorway where Holly had set her down. She hugged Kitty to her chest, and for the first time since Holly snagged her from Brody's grasp, Georgia looked unsettled.

"We are. But probably just for the night. Then we'll have to go back home." Ryan didn't want her to go back to California, but it wasn't just a matter of her protection that she was thinking of. There were obligations. She had a contract waiting to be signed. Of course she had to go back to California. She'd come back to Garnett in hopes of finding some sort of sign to guide her about the new contract. Brody had given her a sign, that was for sure. And if he were to track them down to California, she didn't want to be stuck without the money again.

There was a lull between calls, so she texted Georgia's agent again.

How's the negotiation going? Good, I hope? $$$$

Good not great. But I'm working on it.

"Come on, do your thing," Holly said, tapping the phone against her forehead a few times. "Get the money."

You sure you won't take the offer that's on the table as is? It's a solid offer.

Holly shook her head as if that could translate over text.

Positive. No raise, no Icefall.

Icefall was an international star. If she held out long enough, they would have to offer more money. They would shower her with money if she so much as hinted that Georgia might have something better to do than be their super girl. She had to believe that.

She just needed them to at least offer enough for her to give Brody what he wanted, and then she and Georgia would be free.

Who am I kidding? I'll never be free. I'll give him what he wants, and he'll only want more.

"I don't want to go home yet," Georgia said.

"I don't either," Holly said. She unzipped her bag and rooted around an inside pocket until she found the caramels she'd packed in there back in California. She pulled one out and offered it to Georgia, who took it with a smile. "But we'll come back…someday. Or maybe Nana Cheryl will come see us? Wouldn't that be fun?"

"What about him?" Georgia pointed at the wall that separated their room from Ryan's. "Will he come see us, too?"

"Ryan? I mean, Mr. Oldham? I don't think so."

"He's nice, I think. You should invite him over for dinner at our house. You could make pancakes. I bet he likes pancakes, and you make really good ones."

Holly's heart warmed. Georgia was such a sweet little girl. Pancakes were her favorite food, so wanting to share them with someone was a big deal. "California is a long way from Kansas. That's an awful long drive for pancakes."

"But you could make his pancake look like a smiley face, like you do for me. Then he'd probably want to come."

"You're right, sweetie. He would probably like smiley-face pancakes."

Georgia hopped on her toes. "I'll tell him!"

There was a tap on the window. Ryan stood on the other side, his backpack slung over one shoulder. For a fleeting moment, Holly allowed herself the one fantasy that had held her up for so long: Ryan was hers and she his and they were happy together, a perfect fit. In that moment, they were on a fun little vacation. A road trip with their daughter. They would stop for breakfast and do some silly touristy things and look all over for the perfect souvenirs and take loads and loads of smiling, happy photos.

Except that Holly knew that not only would her fan-

tasy never happen, but that she'd missed out on it because she'd never made her feelings known. She felt
dashed. To know that he shared the fantasy and the
feelings, but that they'd both given up on each other,
was sour and deflating.

Georgia threw open the door. "Do you like smiley-
face pancakes?"

Ryan stepped back, surprised, and chuckled. "Sure
do! Do you?"

Georgia did a funky little dance step in a circle
around him. "They're my favorite. Mommy will make
you some if you come to California. She makes really
good ones, too."

He gave Holly a curious smile and she shrugged.
No doubt about it, she would make him pancakes if he
came to California. But he would never come, and they
both knew that was probably for the best.

"Ready?" he asked, bailing her out of the uncom-
fortable situation.

"Yep. Gee, let's go. Make sure you have Kitty." Holly
reached for Georgia, who took her hand and hopped
toward the car. Holly was exhausted and defeated and
worried and guilty, and she knew Ryan felt the same.

Not exactly the fantasy she'd had in mind.

They piled into Ryan's car, Georgia looking small
and fragile in the back seat without a booster. In their
haste to go after Brody, Holly had never even considered that she would need a booster seat to get her
back home.

"I'll take it slow and careful," Ryan said when he
saw Holly assessing the back seat, biting her lip. She

nodded. She knew she could trust him. "Unless you want to stop somewhere and buy one?"

Her phone lit up again. She shook her head. "Let's just go. We've got to get out of here while we still can."

TWELVE

It was true. Georgia never stopped talking and singing. But Ryan didn't mind. It was a comforting sound.
A sound of family. She was a sweet girl, the spitting
image of her mother, and he could see why a director
would want to work with her, why moviegoers fell in
love with her.

He couldn't, for the life of him, see how Brody could
do anything that could possibly harm her.

But there were a lot of things Brody Shipley did that
Ryan couldn't understand.

They weren't far down the road when the singing
tapered off into silence. He checked the back seat in
the rearview mirror.

"She's asleep," he said.

"I figured. I'm sure she's worn out." Holly's voice
was wooden.

"You okay?"

Holly stared at the passing scenery outside her window. "Not really. I'm exhausted, too. And I've got a
long drive ahead of me. Feels a little daunting."

"You can't even stay one night to get some rest?"

"Not while Brody is still out there. I can't do that to my mom. She's finally built a life meant just for her. She's happy. He knows where she lives, and he's clearly not afraid of showing up there and pushing her around. I can't have him doing that. I also can't risk him getting in and taking Georgia again. I have to get away from him, hide as best I can."

"And what happens if he manages to find you in California?"

"I'll be okay."

Ryan didn't know how much he believed that. Or how much she believed it herself. "You know he's not going to give up, right? Not after coming this close. He's angry."

She checked her phone. Not only was it continually buzzing, but it looked to Ryan like she was waiting for a return call or text as well. "I think I'll give him what he wants."

"I thought you didn't have the money."

"I don't. But Georgia's agent is working on that."

"So you're going to let her be in the new movie?"

He saw tears well up in Holly's eyes, but she blinked them away and turned back to her window, her phone in her lap. "I don't think I have a choice. I came out here for clarity, and I got clarity."

Ryan remembered that Holly was stubborn; he just didn't remember her being this stubborn. He'd tried, and failed, to change her mind. It wasn't going to work. So he had to go with the next best approach. "I can show you some quick self-defense techniques just in case you should need them, okay?"

"Okay. Sure."

"Will you at least stay in touch?"

"Of course," she said, but there was something about the way she said it that made him doubt it was true. "I know you don't think I should go, but I have to do what's best for Georgia and me."

"I know."

"You have to understand that. I'm the person she looks to for stability and safety. Me."

"I know."

"So…" She trailed off, lost in thought or without anything to say, he wasn't sure.

So stay. Let me protect you. Be with me. You don't have to do it alone.

His heart was saying all the things his brain knew he couldn't say. Part of him wondered if her heart was saying the same. If she, too, were wrestling with holding back her feelings.

For the next hour, they rode along in silence, the only sound the pestering buzz of Holly's phone.

Finally, she sighed, picked up the phone and answered it on speaker.

"What, Brody?"

"Once again, you're too dumb for your own good," Brody growled. His voice had a different, more dangerous tone to it than it did before, amped up by fury and recklessness. "It's not possible for you to win this. You can ignore my calls all you want, but you will never lose me. You will never outrun or outsmart or outguess me. Do you understand what I'm saying? You won't get away. I've been following you for miles."

Ryan checked his rearview mirror, just as he'd done dozens of times over the last hour. And just as the dozens of times before, there was no blue truck back there. Just a silver Chevy.

With one person inside it.

Ryan looked closer, kicking himself for not looking closer sooner.

That person was Brody.

"He changed cars again," Ryan said. *And this one looks like it could chase us down.*

Somehow, he'd gotten his hands on another car. He'd been following them unnoticed. They were tired and overwhelmed and they'd gotten Georgia back. And in the midst of all that, they'd lost their vigilance. And here he was. Making her escape impossible. Keeping her on the phone, so she couldn't even call the police to let them know that he was back.

"I'm trying to get the money," Holly said. Her throat was dry and scratchy, the weariness having seeped into every inch of her. "But I won't have it right away. You have to know that. Nobody can just produce five million dollars, even if they have it just sitting around. Surely you understand that."

"I don't have to understand anything," Brody said. "What *you* have to understand is that you've missed your chance. The deal is off the table."

"There was no deal," Ryan said. Holly glanced at him. He had both hands on the steering wheel, his eyes darting to the rearview mirror time and again. She could see in her own side mirror that Brody was inching up on them. Even though Ryan was accelerating, Brody was keeping up with the pace.

"I'm not talking to you. *Cop.* Thought I wouldn't figure it out, huh? *Cop.* Thought you guys were being so smart. But how many times do I have to tell you, Holly, you're dumber than you look."

So he knew. This made Brody even more dangerous.

"I gave you two rules. One, you had twenty-four hours to get me the cash. And, two, no cops. You failed at both. So there is no more deal. Now you just deal with me."

"Ryan is a friend," she said. "He just happens to be a police officer, but that's not why he's helping me."

"It doesn't matter!" Holly had heard this shout from Brody many times before, always when he was at his most dangerous. She began to fear he was hanging on to his sanity by a thread. Maybe he'd already lost it. "Here's what's going to happen, Holly. I'm going to kill you, and Georgia's career is going to take off with me in charge. You've done a terrible job with it, just like you've done a terrible job at everything you've ever done. But I'm here to clean up your mess. As usual."

Holly could feel her own anger bubble up, laced with fear and adrenaline. Maybe, just maybe, she could be as dangerous as he was, if she put her mind to it. Or maybe she could at least make him think she was. "You won't be able to do anything, Brody. I'm the one who signs the contracts. I will just take her and disappear, and there will be no more contracts. You'll have nothing to manage."

"Ding, ding, ding! You've finally got one thing right!

You'll disappear. I'll make sure that happens. You'll just disappear without her."

"Don't listen to him, Holly," Ryan said. "His threats are empty."

"Oh, they're so much more than threats, cop. They're promises. I will kill you first. And then I'll kill Holly. I'll leave you where nobody will find you for a hundred years. And then I'll be the hero who steps in and cares for his little girl after her mother and her boyfriend so selfishly ran away together. Boo-hoo-hoo, ain't life so sad."

"Hang up," Ryan said.

But Holly's hands were paralyzed around the phone, as if her fingers wanted to move to end the call, but the command got lost between her brain and her hands. What Brody was saying was horrifying. But at least hearing him lay out his plan was more comforting than not knowing what his plan was. "I can't—"

"Hang up," Ryan said again, pressing harder on the gas. "And hang on. We're going to lose him."

It wasn't like Ryan to tell someone else what to do. But the more Brody talked, the more Holly shrank. At the same time, he could sense her temperature rising beside him, as she took in the indignity of what he was saying to her.

He supposed there was only so much abuse someone could take without lashing back.

Holly trusted him, so when he told her the second time to disconnect the call, she nodded and flicked off the phone, then tossed it in the center console.

He grabbed his own phone and pressed 9-1-1, gave

their location and requested backup. He let the call stay live while they drove.

"Is Georgia strapped in good and tight?" he asked, as the nose of Brody's car got so close it disappeared in his rearview mirror.

Holly checked the back seat. "Yes."

"I'll be as careful as I possibly can. If anything crazy happens, you go to her. Don't worry about me. Okay?"

"Okay." She was breathless, frightened.

He punched the gas, the new rattle in his fender growing louder and louder, and then settling on a rapid ticking that seemed to blend in with the sound of the engine. His car could move, he knew that much. It was just a matter of how much this new car that Brody was driving could keep up with them.

So far, he was having no trouble.

But at least this time, Ryan was the one leading the chase, and he had backup coming. Which meant he had the upper hand.

He wove through traffic, switching lanes and then switching again. In and out, through and around. Holly grasped the handle above her door with both hands as the car swayed with the motion. He'd managed to put a car between them and Brody. Now if he could just do that a few more times, they might be in the clear.

But the closer he got to Garnett, the denser the traffic became, which made the driving a little trickier. There was less space between cars, so less space for weaving. Indignant drivers slowed as he approached them and didn't budge out of the left lane, even when he hugged their tail and laid on the horn. He wished they were in a squad car, or at least that he had a cherry for the top. Brody was less concerned about his fellow drivers, though, and drove recklessly through them, gaining ground on Ryan and Holly.

Ryan needed to get out of the thick of things.

The first exit he came upon, he would take. But, unlike Brody, he wouldn't make it so obvious. He would wait until the last possible minute to make that move.

"Hold on," he said when he saw an exit up ahead. Fortunately, there were two cars in the right lane, driving slowly and configured in a way that made them impossible to get between. Perfect.

Holly gave a worried glance into the back seat, where Georgia snoozed, still unaware that anything was going on. Satisfied, Holly readjusted her grip on the handle that hung over her window and gave a confident nod. "Do it."

Ryan pulled even with the lead car, pacing himself so that his front wheels were lined up with theirs. The three cars together formed a little blockade. Brody would not be able to gain any ground if he stayed blocked out of the other lane.

Holly glanced at Ryan, curious and alarmed, but said nothing.

"I've got a plan," he said, his concentration on timing.

Patience, patience, he told himself. Don't get greedy.

But Brody wasn't patient, and he was definitely greedy. He gunned his car and bumped the back of Ryan's. Holly let out a little yelp, and Georgia stirred, but Ryan kept his focus, his arms taut, his car on a straight path. Brody bumped him again, harder this time. Ryan's car tried to fishtail, but he kept it steady.

The exit came closer, the tires eating up the asphalt, inch by inch. Ryan's ankle itched at the ready, his foot twitching to push forward, to feel the resistance of the pedal against the sole of his shoe.

Patient. Be patient.

At last, the ramp was there, just feet in front of them. This was going to be dangerous, and he knew the chance that he messed it up and it all went horribly wrong was about as great as the chance that he'd be successful. But he refused to lose his nerve, drawing on the strength of the woman sitting next to him, her jaw set, her body rigid.

Patience...patience...

Now!

With one last glance in his rearview mirror, Ryan shouted out his location for the dispatcher still live on his phone, and then stomped on the gas. The car roared and lurched forward, Holly's head snapping back against the seat rest. She glanced at the back seat again, and then turned back, steady as a rock.

The tires churned over the asphalt as his car sped forward. He swerved around the front of the car next to him and aimed for the ramp.

Just a little too late.

"Hang on," he said, only milliseconds before the car skidded over the gravelly shoulder and thumped through the grass. He was lifted out of his seat as the tires found their purchase against road again. The tires squealed onto the ramp, the steering wheel wrenching out of Ryan's grip with thumps and bumps.

All four tires on concrete, he pawed at the wheel to get the car under control. One fishtail, and then another in the opposite direction, and then he was steady, driving straight for the stop sign at the top of the ramp. He wasn't going to have time to pause, much less stop.

Holly gasped.

He gritted his teeth as he wrestled the car onto the road, narrowly missing an oncoming car. He'd done it. They were safe and moving forward, and the car was still running and still had all of its tires. The question was—where did he go now?

"There," Holly said, seeming to intuit his question, pointing at a side road. She glanced at his phone. "Uh…uh… Church Road! We're turning left on Church Road!"

Ryan aimed for the outer road and almost had it, when his car took another giant lurch forward.

He only had time to look into his mirror once more.

Brody had managed to stay with him through all of that. He was closer than ever before.

And he wasn't about to stop now.

Brody's face was twisted with rage as he leaned over his steering wheel, as if he could make the car go faster just by leaning into it. One side of his bumper hung low, scraping the ground as they traversed the uneven road. And there was an inexplicable crack in Brody's windshield. Had it been there before?

"Police. Hear them?" Holly asked, and Ryan realized that, yes, he could. He was happy to hear the si-

rens. Now he would have the backup he needed and
could just concentrate on keeping Holly and Georgia
safe.

Brody had started to creep up beside them, veer-
ing so close to the side of their car that Ryan thought
he could have reached out the window and high-fived
him. He was clearly planning to sideswipe. And Ryan's
foot was pressed to the floor. His car was going as fast
as it could—but it wasn't going fast enough. He had
to think. He had to come up with a plan, and quickly.

"Mommy?" he heard from the back seat, and it was
that tiny distraction that ended the chase.

It happened in a blur of sights and sounds that felt
like the universe was unraveling. Holly heard Georgia
call out for her. She turned just in time to see how close
the front of Brody's car was to theirs; he was nearly
side-by-side with them now.

"Ryan! Watch out!" she cried, just as Brody nosed
his car into the side of theirs.

Ryan's arms and hands became a flurry of motion,
trying to right the path of their steering and keep them
on the road. But the road was too narrow, the hit too
hard. There was a little gully on the side of the road—
the kind that a curious and bored child would float
pieces of grass and dried leaves on during a rainy day.
Not deep, but deep enough to swallow a tire if it got
too close.

And they got too close.

She could feel more than see how out of control they
were, skidding all over the road, the gravel pitching

up in ticks and creaks against their doors, hood and windows. The world outside was movement without context, and all Holly could do was reach toward the back seat in a fruitless effort to keep Georgia from moving with it.

If anything crazy happens, you go to Georgia.

By the time the front tire found the gully, lost purchase with asphalt and dipped into the air, Holly had already begun to brace herself for the worst. Still, she reached for Georgia, as if she could brace both of them if she could just touch her daughter.

Georgia reached out to her, and then the world was a tumble of movement. Holly's head hit the window, hard, and tempered glass rained down over her. Her shoulder and hip dug into the seat belt. The top of the car grazed her head, once, twice, then a third time, and trees and sky spun around her. Holly's ears filled with the noise of collision.

The movement stopped, the car slowly swaying into a resting position. Holly had one peaceful moment of not understanding what had happened, what she was seeing, but then realized that the world through the windshield was the wrong direction. She was seeing grass rather than sky, and her shoulder ached from being pressed against the seat belt.

"Are you all right?" Ryan asked, his voice barely stifling a groan. "Holly? Georgia?"

It was in that moment that Georgia shrieked in response, the high-pitched wailing of a startled child whose universe had just been upended.

That was the sound that drove Holly from her stupor.

"I'm okay," she said. "I'm good. I'm just…"

She fumbled around to release her seat belt. She felt her pulse in her eyeballs, and finally understood that they were upside-down.

"Help me get out of this?"

Ryan had freed himself and spun so that he was kneeling on the roof of the car. He reached over and fiddled with Holly's seat belt until she felt release and crumpled onto her shoulder on the roof of the car, pain stabbing her in the ribs, forehead and hip. Georgia's shrieks had turned into jagged cries, the kind of cry that would normally tug at Holly's heart but in the moment, made her grateful. As long as Georgia was crying, she was breathing. And that was the important thing.

"I'm coming, baby. It's okay," she said as she let her knees fall to the roof of the car, somersaulting her so that she was right-side-up. Glass pebbles dug into her skin through her jeans.

"Are you hurt?" Ryan asked, blood dripping down one side of his face.

"Yeah. But I'll be fine. You're bleeding."

He swiped at the blood, wiped his hand on his jeans, then reached into his waistband and found his gun. "I'm okay. I'm going out."

Holly didn't argue. She knew it would be pointless. And, besides, she wanted this to be done as much as Ryan did. Maybe more. She wanted Brody caught and sent to jail. The sirens were coming, but they still weren't close enough. "Be safe. He's dangerous." Understatement of the century.

She watched as Ryan crawled through the shattered windshield, glass crunching beneath his knees.

"Ryan?"

He turned, leaned back down so he was looking in the window.

"Come back to us?"

He nodded once but didn't answer. Just got to his feet and loped away.

"Mom-meee!" Georgia wailed, bringing Holly back to the present. The girl had been tossed around by the movement of the car, but the seat belt had mostly kept her in place. She hung upside down by one leg, looking alarmed but mostly unharmed.

Holly crawled across the roof until she reached her daughter, then swooped her up and cradled her.

"Put your arms around my neck."

"Kittyyy…"

"Georgia, put your arms around my neck."

Georgia reached toward her mother, grabbing with intensity that Holly didn't know her daughter had.

"Okay, now hold on tight. I'm going to unbuckle you."

Georgia did as she was asked, and Holly pressed the button on her seat belt. Fortunately, it gave way, and her daughter flopped into her arms, sobbing so hard she was limp.

Holly couldn't help herself—she cried with her daughter, burying her face into the famous Icefall hair, which also just happened to be the fine, wispy, white-gold locks that smelled like powdery detangler and baby shampoo that she'd come to associate with all the best moments of her life.

She's okay. We're okay. It's okay.

Holly let her hands roam, tweaking elbows and joints and making sure there were no broken parts. Thankfully, Georgia appeared to have no serious injuries.

Holly held her tightly, leaning her head against the seat, grateful for the breeze that flowed in from the shattered back window.

How many times would she thank God for this child's existence?

"It's okay, baby. We're okay. It was just an accident."

But Holly knew it wasn't just an accident. And as long as Brody was still out there, they weren't okay.

"I want out of here," Georgia wailed.

"I know. We will in just a minute—"

Holly felt something in her hair. At first she thought the breeze had intensified but then realized that it was the feeling of something moving in her hair. She loosened her grip on Georgia and tried to sit up straight, but suddenly her hair was yanked, lighting her up with pain, and pulling her head toward the opening where the window had once been.

Holly let out a yelp and her hands flew up to her head, releasing Georgia. She turned her head just enough to see Brody's face, smeared with blood and purple with thunderous rage. He had a handful of her hair and was pulling, pulling, determined to get her out of the car. She grabbed his hands and churned her legs and resisted with all that she had, but he was too strong for her.

He dragged her out through the broken back window and onto the gravel road outside.

She could hear Georgia squealing inside the car, but it was a distant sound, all but drowned out by the ringing in her ears, Brody's huffing and puffing, and her own grunts as she tried everything she could to leverage herself against him.

"Say goodbye, Mommy," Brody seethed into her ear as he stood, drawing her up with him, her entire scalp on fire. He lurched through the gully and yanked her along the grass and into the soy field that they'd crashed into. She tripped and stumbled to her knees, crying out at the wrenching pain in her scalp. "Get up!" He tugged so hard, she thought her hair would simply give. She may have even welcomed it, if it meant the pain would end and she could be free of his grasp. "I said get up, you dumb cow. Hope you gave her a good, long hug, and kissed your boyfriend goodbye. You won't be seeing them again."

She tried not to be dragged down a tunnel of long-buried memories. This was how it always had been between them. He was bigger, stronger and much, much meaner. She was powerless against him, paralyzed by fear and pain. Bending to his will.

Not. Anymore. Not today. Not with Georgia watching.

Surprise. He always had the element of surprise on his side. Why couldn't she use the same tactic? He expected her to resist him, to fight against the movement across the field. If she came at him, he would never see it coming.

So that was exactly what she would do.

* * *

Brody's car was in no better shape than Ryan's. In fact, Brody's car was smoking from under the hood, which was right-side-up, but had rolled. The entire car was dented, balled up like a crumpled tin can, and if Ryan had been pulling up on this scene as an officer, he might have assumed there would be no survivors.

But Ryan wasn't an officer pulling up on an accident scene. He knew Brody well enough to know that he would not only survive the crash but would come out swinging.

He pointed his gun at the car and crept toward it, trigger finger at the ready.

"Come out!" he shouted. A trickle slid down the side of his face, which was otherwise numb from hitting the steering wheel with his cheek. "Hands up and come out!"

But there was no movement from within the crashed car. Only the hiss and smoke of a wreck.

"Brody! I know you hear me. Keep your hands where I can see them and come out!"

Still nothing.

Maybe.

Just maybe...

Maybe Ryan and Holly had gotten lucky, and Brody had been knocked unconscious. There were still sirens in the air; maybe a police car would come upon the scene before he woke up, and they could get him detained and in an ambulance with no fight.

Would they get that lucky?

He doubted it.

Brody Shipley was like a cockroach—he could survive anything.

"Brody!" he called again. "You hear those sirens, right? You might as well give up now. Make it easier on yourself."

He crouched to look inside the car. Brody wasn't there. Ryan blinked in confusion, then stood and went around the back of the car, to the ditch on the other side. Maybe Brody had been thrown and was lying somewhere in the soy field.

He started to lower his gun, but then he heard Holly cry out.

Leaked oil had made the grass slippery, and Ryan went down in the gully. But he was up again in a flash and heading toward his car. Because he was certain that he not only heard Holly cry out, but he heard the sounds of a scuffle on gravel.

Brody was fast—Ryan would give him that much. He had two fistfuls of Holly's hair and had already dragged her out of the car and was moving at a steady clip across the field, with Holly in tow.

"Holly!" Ryan shouted, bolting toward them. "Let her go or I'll shoot!"

Brody called his bluff. "You won't shoot. You might shoot her."

He was right. Ryan wouldn't shoot toward that kind of scuffle for that reason. But nobody said he couldn't rush the guy and take him down.

Only—Holly beat him to it.

Brody had slowed just slightly. It was just enough pause for Holly to stretch her arms out straight and rush right into him, driving Brody to the ground. They both landed with an *oof* that Ryan heard all the way from where he was. One of Brody's hands loosened from Holly's hair. She began pounding on his arm, trying to get him to let go with the other hand. And it worked.

Holly fell backward, landing on her backside in the dirt, and dug her feet into the ground to push herself backward, away from Brody. Her chest heaved with ragged breaths, and her hair hung in her face. She glanced back at the car, where Georgia's cries could still be heard, and back at Brody, afraid to let him out of her sight for more than a second. Back and forth, back and forth, her legs pushing her away the entire time.

Ryan wanted to go to her.

But he was more enraged than ever. Brody Shipley would not get away today if Ryan had anything to do with it. Brody locked eyes with him, and in a single instant, seemed to understand what Ryan intended to do. He scrambled to his feet.

The next thing Ryan knew, Brody was half lurching, half running through the field.

Ryan crammed the gun back into his waistband holster and followed, the twinges of battered spots on his own body thrumming, but the adrenaline and determination coursing through him were too strong for him to care.

Brody was heading for some woods nearby, likely hoping to lose Ryan the way he lost him earlier in the morning in the cornfield.

But as Holly's courageous face appeared in his mind, he became even more resolved that there was no way he could allow that to happen. He had to end this. Now.

The police sirens had gotten much closer, much louder, and he hoped the officers were paying attention. He didn't have time to flag them down. He would lose Brody if he so much as turned his head, he was certain of that. But he heard Holly yelling and imagined that she was headed back toward the road, flagging them down herself.

The little oasis of trees was getting closer and closer with every step. Ryan's muscles and lungs burned as he stretched each stride wider and wider, closing the gap between himself and Brody. He imagined himself running back through time, to the moment where Brody appeared onto the scene and stole his future away from him. He imagined closing the distance to Brody just as young Brody reached for young Holly's hand. He imagined himself swooping between the outstretched hands, blocking them, grabbing Holly around the waist and spinning her, her head thrown back in delighted laughter, and Brody simply...fading away.

He was close enough to hear Brody breathing, to hear the soft crunch of soy plants as his feet landed, *one-two, one-two, one-two*. Brody's limp had gotten more pronounced, and now Ryan was close enough to see blood dripping down the back of Brody's head.

He powered forward, his feet moving so quickly, they almost felt like they left the ground. And then they did. Ryan got just close enough to reach Brody in one great leap. The two landed in a jumble of limbs, surrounded by soy plants and yellowed grass, the shade of the nearby trees mottling their skin.

"Get…off…of…me…" Brody panted, trying to wrestle his way out from under Ryan. He was as strong as Ryan expected him to be.

"Stop moving," Ryan warned. "You're done. You've gone far enough." He meant this on just about every level. They'd traveled far enough to bring this to an end. Brody had also taken advantage of Georgia and Holly far enough. Had taken the chase far enough. Had tested Ryan's patience far enough.

This was done.

Brody wasn't going to give up easily, though. He writhed and panted and grunted and squirmed beneath Ryan. Finally, Ryan was able to get his hand around to his holster. He pulled the gun, rose up on his knees, and pointed it directly at Brody.

"I said freeze."

To his surprise, Brody did. He lay nestled in the weeds, panting, his hands up by his ears.

"I…deserve the money…and you know it," he said, his breath slowing.

The sirens grew deafening. There was the sound of a spray of gravel, some shouting and a tremble in the earth as officers raced in.

"The only thing you deserve is jail," Ryan said. "And I'm going to make sure you get there and stay there until Georgia is old enough to kick you out of her life herself."

"She won't…want to. She…loves me."

"She loves the man you should be, not the man you are. Just like Holly did."

Brody smirked. "Ah… I get it—now," he panted. "You think…this will make… Holly love you…don't you? You're wrong… She will never…love you."

"This isn't about me," Ryan said. "It's about you being done."

"Drop your weapon! Drop your weapon!"

Ryan tossed his gun to the side and put his hands up, never breaking eye contact with Brody. "It's over," he said, lacing his fingers behind his head. "Whether or not she loves me, she won't have to worry about you anymore. That's all I need."

The shouts got closer, and now Ryan could hear the officers' footsteps, not just feel them. They approached with guns pointed. Ryan braced himself to be taken down and cuffed, and watched through the grass, barely feeling the metal hugging his own wrists, as an officer approached Brody and expertly flipped him to his stomach. Within moments, Brody's hands were cuffed behind his back, and they were both being pulled to their feet.

The officers marched both men to the cruisers and searched them. Ryan explained who he was and what had happened and was grateful when one of his colleagues recognized him and removed the handcuffs. Ryan leaned against the cruiser, catching his breath, while listening to an officer read Brody his rights.

"You okay?" the officer asked.

"Yeah. I'm good." This wasn't entirely true. Ryan hated how Brody had gotten to the heart of his single greatest failure. He was wrong on one thing, though— Ryan thought Holly could have loved him. But he was right in that Ryan would never get to know. Holly had made her decision, and he wasn't her choice.

"Your car, though, man. Too bad you weren't in a squad."

Ryan and the officer turned to face the road. Ryan's car was destroyed. But all three of them were alive. Maybe God sometimes had a way of answering prayers that weren't even prayed.

Holly stood next to the wreckage, Georgia on one hip, talking to an EMT, nodding, answering questions. Protocol.

"Thank God everyone survived," the officer said.

Ryan nodded. "My thoughts exactly."

Holly followed the EMT to the ambulance, Georgia limp and warm in her arms, her cries having been drowned into silence by the sirens and ensuing bustle. Still, she kept her arms around Holly's neck.

"Take her first," Holly said, handing Georgia over to the paramedic. "I think she's fine, but I want to double-check."

Georgia whimpered in protest, but went to the lady without a fight, once again displaying the maturity Holly had grown to know and love in her daughter, even if she hated the fact that Georgia had to have that maturity to do what was expected of her.

"Oh, is this your kitty cat?" the paramedic asked.

"Yeah."

"What's her name?"

"Kitty."

A chuckle. "That's a great name. Do you think I should check out Kitty first?"

Georgia smiled and nodded. "I think she hurt her nose."

"Oh, no. A hurt nose. I don't know how that feels. Do you?"

Holly let them fade away as she searched for Ryan through what had become a crowd of emergency personnel. Brody had wanted no police and had ended up with what looked like the entire forces of two different towns, plus highway patrol. Served him right.

She saw two officers pushing Brody into the back of a squad car, and at last she found Ryan behind them. He looked tired. Winded. A bit defeated.

His car, she thought. It's ruined. He could have died. He did this for me.

For me.

After all these years pining, he risked everything for me.

She waited for him to look up, to search for her the way she was searching for him.

"Mommy, Kitty got a banged-aid. See? Her nose is broken."

Georgia was sitting on the end of the stretcher, legs happily swinging. She held up Kitty, who had a bandage stuck across the bridge of its nose.

"She sure did, Gee. Is she okay?"

"Going to be just fine," the EMT said. "Now let's take a look at you."

Holly let herself be pulled into the back of the ambulance with Georgia, giving one last long glance back before ducking all the way in.

At last, Ryan looked up at her. He gave one nod that sent tingles down her spine.

He had risked everything for her.

Yet, here she was, walking away. Alone.

"I'd prefer to have you both checked out at the hospital," the EMT said.

"Sure. Yeah. That's fine," Holly said. She sank gratefully onto the stretcher next to Georgia, her legs weak and shaky.

The paramedics closed the door, and they pulled away before Holly could so much as give Ryan a *thank-you*.

A final thought came to her as they bumped along the road back to the highway.

Maybe leaving is the best thank-you I can give him.

THIRTEEN

"Unbelievable," Cheryl said as she pawed through the curtain to get into the ER bay where Holly and Georgia sat on a bed, shoes on and ready to go. "I saw the car. I almost can't believe you're okay." She hugged Holly and Georgia both in one swoop of her arms and then pulled back. "You are okay, right?"

"We're okay," Holly confirmed. "Got some bumps and bruises, and we're a little sleepy but otherwise very fortunate. Considering."

"What about Ryan?"

Holly shrugged. "I haven't talked to him. But he seemed mostly unharmed in the moment, at least."

"And…the other?"

"Also seemed fine. But I definitely haven't talked to that one. And won't be talking to him anytime soon. Or ever."

Cheryl sat on the chair opposite them and laid her purse in her lap, looking prim and proper. "Can't say I blame you there."

The curtains bubbled and in slipped a nurse, a clipboard in hand. "Okay, you two. Got you all cleared to go. Remember to take it easy for a couple of days. You're probably going to be a little sore. Use it as an excuse to do nothing but lay around the pool and read books." She winked at Holly.

If only.

Had Holly not been so numb with fatigue at this point, she might have found it in herself to feel jealous of the people who got to do that sort of thing. That had never been her life, and she doubted it was about to start to be that way now.

Brody was detained, but she had no way of knowing what the future would hold. Would he post bail and be released immediately? And what would happen if he were to make a plea or get probation or quickly serve his time—would he just come right after her again?

"You ready?" Cheryl asked, snapping Holly out of her daydream.

"Huh? Yeah. Let's go. Come on, Gee." Holly stretched her hand out and Georgia took it. She looked just as sleepy as Holly felt, and she'd stopped chattering and singing. A sure sign that she'd been pushed to her limit.

She'll be asleep before we leave the parking lot, Holly thought.

As soon as she ducked into the car, her phone buzzed in her back pocket. A pang of fear resonated through her, and she had to remind herself that there was no way it was Brody. Not yet, anyway. She dug the phone out. The screen was shattered, barely usable. She ran her thumb over the roughness and sighed. She really couldn't afford a new phone right now.

Her sigh turned into a giggle, and then a laugh.

Cheryl looked at her curiously. "What's so funny?"

Holly wiped tears from the corners of her eyes and shook her head. "Nothing." How could anyone understand the irony of what she'd just been through, given that she didn't even have enough cash to fund a bottom-of-the-line phone? As if she'd ever been able to scrape up the kind of money Brody was looking for. She would have promised him the moon, if that was what it took to get Georgia back. She was just as likely to be able to give him that as she was the money.

She wiped her eyes again and squinted at the screen. She'd missed a call, and what was buzzing was a voicemail. She held it to her ear, secretly hoping that it was Ryan.

It wasn't.

"Hi, Holly, it's Lynne. Just wanted to let you know that I've talked to the *Precipitators* execs until I'm blue in the face, and they won't budge. They swear that Icefall is a replaceable character. Now, we all know Georgia is a delight and nobody could ever replace her, and that any time these Hollywood folks get it into their heads that they can just sub out a beloved character without anyone knowing or caring, they are dead wrong. I mean, *Bewitched*? Darrin? Am I right? Ah, you're too young to know what I'm talking about. Anyway, so I was thinking there's one more tactic I can use…" Holly pulled the phone away from her ear and thumbed it off. Good thing Lynne was thinking, because Holly's brain was totally fried. But she did understand the *Bewitched* reference, no matter how young she was.

She laid her head back on the seat and dozed off with one last thought. *What was so wrong, really, with the second Darrin...?*

Stitches were a hassle. Ryan tried to convince the ER doctor that he didn't need them, but she wasn't having it.

"Don't be petulant. It will only take minutes." She tapped her clipboard against the seat, indicating that he was to sit there.

There's no shortage of clipboards around this place.

In the end, he sat, not because he was afraid of scarring, as she tried to convince him he should be—it was, after all, a small spot high up on his temple that nobody would ever notice anyway—but because his legs were too tired to keep standing.

Adrenaline had a way of deciding for you that you're done.

"So, tell me what happened here," the doctor said, swabbing something cold and wet over his skin.

"Car accident," he said.

"You hit the window?"

"And the door and the roof and the seat belt and the dashboard."

She sucked in a breath through her teeth. "Yikes, sounds like you rolled it."

"A few times, yeah."

"This is going to sting just a little. So you obviously hit your head. Have you gone through concussion protocol?"

"Yes," he said, a little white lie. One of the other officers had him follow his fingers around in his line of sight. Nothing wonky happened, so they both declared him concussion-free.

"And?"

"All good."

She was silent for a beat. Ryan's skin tugged this way and that, but he felt no pain. "You must feel very fortunate."

"I got the bad guy," he said. "That was all I was looking to do."

Not true. You were also looking to get the girl, and you spectacularly failed at that.

"Well, thank you for getting a bad guy off the streets. Just a few more here, and then you can go." She was silent while she finished yanking around on his skin and then tossed her instruments onto a little pad on a table next to her, before standing up. She pulled off her gloves. "Some of my best work. You'll never know anything was there."

"Thank you," he said. "Can I...can I just keep lying here for a minute, though?"

She peered down at him, her brow creased. "Are you dizzy?"

"No. I just—it feels good to rest." *And I think I have some inside work to do.*

"I see. How about you just relax while I get your paperwork? I'll write slowly. But if you insist on being horizontal after I come back, I'm going to insist on an official concussion assessment."

"Deal."

He closed his eyes before she even left the room,

and instantly Holly's face filled his vision. He'd gotten word that she and Georgia were unharmed. At first, he was going to track them down and make sure, to see it with his own eyes, but something made him pull back. He'd gone through a lot to protect her from Brody, that was true. And he was almost certain that he would've done the same for anyone. It was his job, after all.

But he wasn't 100 percent certain, and that was the part that messed with him.

He had told himself he was done pining for her. And he'd thought he really was. But clearly, he wasn't.

Still. He did have a lot to be grateful for. And maybe it was time to reopen that conversation with God. Maybe thank Him for answering prayers that weren't even coming to Him. As an officer, Ryan did witness a lot of inexplicably bad things happen to good people. But he'd also seen good things happen. And, even if he didn't get exactly what he wanted—well, that didn't mean he didn't get exactly what he needed.

How was he supposed to know what was in store for him? That was the faith part of faith—believing that, in the end, you would be exactly where you were meant to be.

He heard the curtain slide on its metal tracks and let one eye drift open.

"That was fast," he said, before he realized it wasn't the doctor coming back in.

"What can I say? I'm speedy." Savannah stood over him, her arms crossed. "You look like you've been in a fight. With a car."

He chuckled. It hurt his ribs. "But I won."

"I ran into some of the guys. They said you got him. Brody Shipley?"

"I did."

"Great job, little brother. But can you, like, just stick with giving out traffic tickets or something for a while? I'm tired of having to start every conversation with Mom with, *Before I say anything, Ryan's okay.* Even all the way down in Florida, she hears everything." She held out a hand. Ryan regarded it at first, but then took it and let her help him sit up.

"Thanks," he said. The sudden elevation made his head throb. "I wasn't officially on duty, though." He swiveled to sit sideways on the bed, his legs dangling off. Savannah scooted up on the bed next to him.

"Ah, that's right. You were helping a friend."

"I was."

"But you were definitely not getting in too deep with a woman you've been in love with since you were twelve."

"Brody had kidnapped their daughter."

"Not a denial. You know, you could just tell her that you still love her."

"What happened to 'protect your heart, Ryan'?"

She bumped his shoulder with her shoulder. "That doesn't always mean shut it down, you know. Protecting your heart could mean following it, too. Don't be so literal."

"It's not what you meant." He returned the shoulder bump, which nosed another bruise into the forefront of his awareness. Getting out of bed tomorrow was going to be interesting.

She chuckled. "You're right, it wasn't. But I thought about it after we hung up. Holly Hampton is a good person. And you're a good person when you're around her."

"I'm a good person all the time."

"Don't miss the point, Mr. Pedantic. Anyway, maybe you two good people should stick together. You obviously have a connection. Why fight it? Why can't letting your heart be full be a way of protecting it, too?"

"You're getting soft in your old age, sis."

"I'm not old."

The curtain slid open again, and a nurse came in. Savannah slid off the bed.

"I'll go pull the car around. We can talk more on the way home."

"Oh, good. I love it when my taxi driver lectures me."

She shrugged. "If your taxi driver is wise to the ways of the world, maybe you should listen to her."

"Isn't *wise* another word for *old*?"

She spun and disappeared. He heard her voice fade as she walked away. "Be careful, or you might find yourself walking home, young'un."

Ryan smiled, and now he could feel swelling in his bottom lip … . He hadn't stopped by a mirror since this all went down, but he must have looked pretty rough.

The nurse went over his paperwork with him. He nodded and pretended to follow along, but all he could think about was Savannah's advice.

He'd tried protecting his heart from Holly for so long. It always seemed like the best move—keep out the woman who could utterly break him—but now he wondered if protecting his heart could mean letting Holly in.

Of course, that would only work if she wanted to be let in.

And right now she was still reeling over Brody.

The advice might have been right, but the timing was all off. Again.

FOURTEEN

Georgia's things were presumably still in Brody's car. Not that she cared. She had Kitty—the only possession that she didn't want to lose.

Still, she needed clothes, and Holly's mom desperately wanted to take them shopping.

"You sure you don't want to stay?" Cheryl asked as they pawed through a rack of sundresses. "We've hardly gotten to visit at all."

"I want to stay," Holly said, "but I told you—the studio offered a good deal, even if it wasn't exactly the one that I wanted. I can't turn it down." Holly pulled a dress out, studied it, shoved it back in. "If I invest it right, Georgia will be set for a good, long time. Plus, I'll have more money in case…" She trailed off, not wanting to even think about repeating the ordeal she just went through. "It's just a good business move for Georgia."

"She's five. She doesn't have business moves."

Holly paused with her hand on a dress. "Mom. You remember what it's like, not having any money, doing it all alone. I don't want Georgia to ever have to wonder if she'll have enough money for groceries or to pay her gas bill or, I don't know, maybe go to the movies every now and then."

"I know, I know. But does she like it?"

"She doesn't dislike it." At least she'd never said so if she did.

Cheryl put her hands up in surrender. "Okay. You win. But can you stay one more day at least? Let me spoil you a little?"

Holly groaned in defeat. She had to admit, she'd so looked forward to this time with her mom, she was disappointed that she would have to leave without doing so. "I wouldn't mind having one more day to rest. But I want to be out of here before Brody can post bail."

"Ryan says he doesn't think he'll have the chance. He has a place to run to in the middle of Arkansas and was actively running there with Georgia, so they think he's a flight risk."

Holly paused. "You talked to Ryan? When?"

"This morning, when you were still sleeping. He was out painting the doorframe. He asked about you."

"He's okay?"

They moved on to another rack of dresses. "He's a little scraped and bruised. Got some stitches. He said he's sore, but otherwise doesn't seem any worse for wear. Oh, this is cute." She tossed a lavender sundress into the cart. "You should talk to him before you go."

Holly went back to sorting through the clothing. "I don't want to bother him."

"Holly…"

"Mom…"

"Oh, look at this one, Georgia! It has kitties on it!" Cheryl waved a dress in front of Georgia. "Speaking of, I thought maybe Nana would get her a new K-I-T-T-Y for the trip home. That one's looking a little raggedy."

Georgia's eyes lit up. "A new kitty?"

Holly laughed. "She can spell some words, Mom. Especially her favorites."

"Would your kitty like a friend?" Cheryl smoothed Georgia's hair and sighed. "Oh, I wish you guys were staying."

Holly did, too. She'd been going on the assumption that Brody would be out soon. That he might be denied bail never dawned on her. But, while that relieved her, it still didn't make sense for her to stay. She couldn't explain why, not even to herself.

"I've already told Jim I would be back at the store on Monday," she said.

They tossed a few more items into the cart, then headed over to the toy section, which was rowdy with children and one tired-sounding mom repeatedly getting after them. It was a voice that Holly thought she recognized but couldn't quite place, until it was saying her name.

"Holly?"

Brenda Shipley stood in the aisle, a child in the basket of her cart, another balanced on the handle rather than sitting in the seat. Holly's first instinct was to bolt. But then she remembered that she'd done nothing wrong and had no reason to run away.

"Is that Brody's kid?"

Holly found herself stepping defensively between

Brenda and Georgia, as if Brenda pointing at her would somehow harm her.

"Let's go find a kitty," Cheryl whispered, and wheeled Georgia away.

"Yes," Holly said. "That's Georgia."

"She looks just like that kid in the *Precipitators* movie."

Holly didn't respond. While Brenda and Brody might not be close, she was still a Shipley, and Holly still didn't trust her.

"So you obviously found her. Were they at the cabin?"

"So you knew they might be and didn't tell me?"

Brenda shrugged. "I didn't know anything for sure. Like I said, Brody didn't say anything to me about a kid."

"We caught up with them before they could get to the cabin," Holly said.

"Brody go on down by himself, then?"

"Brody's in jail, where he belongs," Holly said. There was a crash the next aisle over, followed by a child's cry.

Brenda glanced in that direction, then turned her attention back to Holly. "Jail?" For the briefest moment, vulnerability crossed Brenda's face. She looked sad, regretful. The Shipleys were hardly a close family, but in that moment, Holly thought she could see a wish on Brenda's face that maybe they could have been, if only things were different.

Still, that didn't change the fact that Brody was exactly where he needed to be. "Sounds like no bail for him. He kidnapped a child."

Brenda nodded pensively. "I mean, it was his own

child…" From the next aisle, there were sounds of slapping and grunting, and the wailing got louder. "Stop it, you two!" Brenda shouted. She started to turn her cart around but stopped. "Take care of yourself, Holly."

Holly nodded. She noticed, after Brenda left, that her hands were clammy and shaking.

"Mommy, I got Kitty a friend!"

Cheryl pushed the cart toward Holly. Georgia sat in the seat and held the stuffed cat high.

"His name's Catty."

Holly smiled. Such a sweet girl. "Catty?"

"Kitty and Catty!"

There was such joy on Georgia's face and matching joy on Cheryl's that Holly started to doubt her decision to leave. What would it hurt, really, to stay two more days? Or five? Ryan lived next door, but it wasn't like he would be impossible to avoid.

If, of course, she wanted to avoid him.

One more day turned into two and then three. Holly couldn't bring herself to leave, even though she knew she needed to. She felt peace here, tranquility. Her mom was the comfort that she needed.

But she would be lying to herself if she didn't also say that Ryan was part of why she stayed, too. She hadn't talked to him since he crawled out of the wrecked car, but she'd wanted to. Oh, she'd wanted to.

Where did she start, exactly?

I love you, but I can't. I've always loved you, but I wasted it. I don't want to leave you, but I'm leaving.

Some chances were just missed, and that was that.

She did find herself, however, sitting at the kitchen table quite often, chin propped on hand, watching Ryan through the sliding glass door as he went about his business. Occasionally, she watched him pull weeds and imagined him picking a bouquet for her and handing it over the fence. Or, sometimes, she simply imagined their hands entwined, their palms pressed together, as they sat on the back porch and watched the sunset.

Those were things she never imagined of Brody. Because Brody would never do them. And even if he did, she didn't want them from him. Brody was excitement and danger, not sunsets and smiles.

Why don't you go outside and talk to him? Cheryl had asked on more than one occasion, and Holly had simply shaken her head. Her mother knew her all too well. She knew that Holly was pining, and she also knew that, even if she suggested it a thousand times, Holly would never again go to that fence. At least not until it stopped hurting.

Which was probably going to be never.

But tonight, Ryan wasn't in the backyard, and when Georgia yelled, *Come on, Mommy! You can help us pick tomatoes, too!* she gave in. She followed Georgia, lagging behind as she soaked in the warmth of the early evening summer sun and listened to the cicadas begin singing another chorus of their song. Her mom really had done a lovely job with the yard.

"Mommy, over here!"

Holly followed the stone path that led to the garden and found Georgia ducked down low between two plants.

"Look," Georgia whispered. "A worm. He's fuzzy. Isn't he cute?" She used one sticky little finger to poke at a caterpillar that was lazily crawling along a leaf.

"He is cute," Holly said. "Let's not poke him, though. This is his house. You wouldn't like it if someone came into your house and poked you."

"I'm gonna do more than poke at these tomato worms," Cheryl said from over behind a tomato plant. "Nasty little things."

"I wanna see it! Come on, Mommy, let's go see the worm." Georgia skipped off.

Holly straightened. She didn't really want to see a tomato worm, thank you very much, and especially if her mother was going to do more than poke it, as she said. Holly put her hands on her waist and arched her back, stretching. Seemed she was always stiff since the wreck. She would probably need to have that looked at eventually.

"Mommy! Come see!"

Holly started to give in when something whizzed over her head and landed right on the bush in front of her. She ducked and took a minute to figure out what had just flown past.

It was a Frisbee.

He'd found it in his garage, buried in a bin filled with relics of his childhood. Basketballs, tennis rackets, jump ropes, a beach towel, and a Frisbee.

Actually...*the* Frisbee.

He had no explanation for why he pulled it out of the bin, or why he brought it into the house, or why he placed it on his coffee table. Or why he couldn't help but sit and stare at it every time he sat on his couch.

Contemplating.

Remembering.

Ruminating.

In the end, it was the words he'd said to Brody as they'd walked him to the squad cars that made his decision for him.

Why are you helping her, man? Brody had asked.

Ryan had responded with a question of his own. *How could you walk away from her?*

Brody had turned, grinned like he'd just stumbled upon a secret too delicious to pass by. He arched one eyebrow. *So that's why, huh? You're a fool. She's nothing.*

But the way Ryan saw it, Brody was the foolish one. He'd let the most beautiful, kindest, sweetest woman in the world slip through his fingers.

And that was what Ryan thought about while staring at the Frisbee.

Wasn't he doing the same thing, after all? Letting her slip through his fingers? And why? Because he was scared?

He would jump into a burning building for her. He would step in front of a speeding train for her. He would climb out of a smoking car, still seeing double, and chase a criminal full-on through a soy field. For her.

But he was afraid of loving her.

It was ridiculous.

He moved the Frisbee to the kitchen table. Had dinner with it.

And then she'd appeared outside.

It was the first time he'd seen her since the accident. Not that he'd been avoiding her, but—well, he had been avoiding her. And he suspected that she'd been avoiding him.

But here she was, wandering around in her mother's garden, wearing a white sundress that glowed like her hair when the sun hit it. She was barefoot. She was smiling. She was with Georgia.

"Brody, you're right," Ryan said aloud at his dinner table. "I've been a fool."

He stood, grabbed the Frisbee, and stepped outside. He half expected her to hear him or notice him or maybe just in some way intuit him as he stood on his back porch, the Frisbee heavy and meaningful in his hands. But she never turned. He aimed, flicked his wrist and let the Frisbee sail.

It landed in the bush right in front of her. And at last she looked up. He may have been imagining things, but he could have sworn he saw the blue in her eyes all the way from across two lawns. She giggled, shaking her head, then stood and plucked the Frisbee out of the bush.

"Sorry. My bad," he said as she picked her way across the yard toward the fence. "I'm not very good at throwing those."

She used it to fan herself. "Seems to me that it landed exactly where you wanted it to go. Unless, of course, you were aiming for a more specific target." She tapped the plastic lightly against her forehead.

"Nah, not this time. I already got your attention, so I didn't need to."

Her mouth dropped open in surprise. "Are you admitting to me, after all these years, that you're the one who hit me with this Frisbee? And on purpose?" She reached across the fence and playfully whacked his arm with the toy.

"No, no, I'm not saying it was on purpose, *per se*... I'm just saying that I may have been hoping you would turn around so I could get your attention. And when you never did—I lost control of my throw."

"Ryan Thomas Oldham, I can't believe you." She tossed the Frisbee over the fence. It flew over Ryan's head and across the lawn, landing up against the fence on the other side.

He paused, warmth spreading throughout his chest. "You remember my middle name."

"I used it enough times," she said. "Of course I remember it."

"Kay," he said. "Holly Kay Hampton."

She smiled, and for a moment, Ryan thought she might reach across the fence toward him, and that he wouldn't have to admit his feelings at all. That she would just know and share them, and they would be together. But her smile turned sad, and she looked down at her feet.

"Something wrong?" Ryan asked.

"I never thanked you," she said. "I don't know if I would have gotten Georgia back if you hadn't been there."

"Of course. I couldn't have not helped you."

"Serve and protect," she said sadly.

He surprised himself by reaching across the fence

for her hand. It was warm in his. "That's not why I had to help you."

"Ryan…"

"Do you remember what I said in the car? That whole bit about Morgan and how she wasn't the one for me because I was comparing her to you all the time and she just couldn't win?"

"Ryan…"

"Do you remember that I said I wasn't going to long after you anymore, that we were just friends, and it was all good? It isn't. It isn't good, Holly. I am still pining after you. I love you, Holly. I always have. I always will."

"Ryan…" She pulled her hand out of his and crushed his heart with one small step backward. She shook her head, her eyes shining with tears. "I'm going back to California tomorrow."

He felt like he was withering inside. Tumbling backward through the years, hurt all over again. "Stay."

"I can't. I have a life in California."

"I can be part of that life." He sounded desperate, but he didn't care. This was his shot, and he was going to take it, no matter how much it hurt.

"I'm sorry, Ryan. I really am. It's not just my life. It's Georgia's. She's got…obligations."

"No," he said. "That's not it. You're afraid."

"I'm not."

"You are," he said, and he could tell from the look on her face that he was right. She was afraid. And could he really blame her, after all that she'd been through? "You don't have to be afraid with me. I'm not Brody."

"I know that." She bit her lip, which had begun to tremble just slightly. "But there's so much at stake. And if things go wrong…"

"They won't."

"But if they do."

He knew what she was thinking. Brody had been a monster. Abusive. Ugly. Controlling. And, ultimately, he'd abandoned her. She'd spent years getting over that, coming to terms with what she'd been through. Working hard to raise Georgia alone. Of course she was scared. She had every right to be. His mouth opened, but he found that he had nothing to say.

"I'm sorry," she repeated, then hesitated for just a beat before turning and walking away.

"Mommy, we found another tomato worm!" Georgia shouted from within the rows of plants. But Holly didn't respond. She just kept walking.

Out of the backyard.

Into the house.

Out of Ryan's life forever.

FIFTEEN

"You'll call the moment you get there, of course," Cheryl said, hanging over the car door through the open window.

"And when we stop for the night. And any time I might feel sleepy while I'm driving. And if I'm bored or need advice or just want to say hi," Holly intoned, repeating the instructions Cheryl had given her a thousand times.

"And you can call Nana anytime you like," Cheryl said to Georgia, giving her a light pinch on one cheek.

"I really wish you hadn't bought her that," Holly said, nodding to the shiny new cell phone in Georgia's hands that just happened to match Holly's own shiny new cell phone, both going-away presents from her mom. "She's five."

"She has to call her Nana somehow, isn't that right, Georgia?" She gave her granddaughter an exaggerated wink.

"It's got games," Georgia said. Truly, that had been the only thing about the phone that had excited Georgia. Holly supposed she would let her use it to keep herself occupied during the drive, but when they got home to California, it would likely live on a shelf.

"Are you sure you won't stay?" Cheryl tried, for the hundredth time, to change Holly's mind.

"I have to sign the contract first thing Monday," Holly said. "And I have a morning shift."

"Okay, okay, I know. I understand. Well, I'm still planning on coming out there for Christmas, so be ready."

Her mom had made promises to come to California in the past, but had never made good on those promises. In the end, it was just too hard to leave Garnett, even for just a few days.

"We'll have a bed all ready for you. She'll probably be working by then, so it might be kind of busy."

"You can come see the set," Georgia said. "And you'll see my hair get all poofed up." She motioned around her head like there was a cloud on top of it, which, sometimes, was exactly what it looked like when she came out of hair and makeup.

"I can hardly wait," Cheryl said, beaming at her granddaughter.

"We've got to go, Mom," Holly said. "I want to get to Santa Fe before bedtime."

"We're gonna eat tacos in the car, Nana," Georgia said. "Aren't we, Kitty and Catty?" She held up her stuffed toys and made them hop around excitedly in her lap, her new phone already forgotten.

"Okay, okay," Cheryl said. "Just remember to call."

"Right." Holly put the car into gear and gulped back

tears that matched the ones standing in her mother's eyes. "Love you, Mom."

"Love you, too. Both of you." Cheryl stepped back from the car and waved, the knuckles of her other hand pressed against her lips. Unlike Holly, she was terrible at hiding emotion.

Holly backed out of the driveway and swung into the street. She leaned forward to wave at her mother one more time.

And saw Ryan, standing on his porch, his arms crossed, everything about him drawn together tight.

"There's Mr. Ryan," Georgia said. She stuck her little hand out the open window as far as she could reach from her booster seat. "Bye, Mr. Ryan! We're going home now."

Slowly, he raised his hand in a single wave.

But Holly couldn't bear to return it. She put the car into gear and swiftly drove away.

It was a long eleven hours to Santa Fe. They'd eaten tacos and sung along to music and played Kitty and Catty until they were hoarse. They'd stopped for six bathroom breaks and one apple pie break and another break just because Holly needed a minute to get fresh air and stretch her legs.

Georgia didn't whine. Georgia never whined.

The sun had set long ago when they finally pulled up to their hotel in New Mexico. It was impossible to think they'd already gone that far, and they still weren't quite halfway there.

"It's hot," Georgia mumbled as they lugged their

bags into their room. The air conditioner wasn't doing the best job of battling the heat; the room was stuffy.

"We'll take baths to cool off," Holly said.

"Can I watch TV?" Georgia asked, and for a moment, Holly felt transported back to that morning when she'd tucked away in Ryan's room while he went after Brody.

She'd thought of Ryan at least once an hour since they left.

Who was she kidding? She thought of him ten times an hour.

Every little reference—*Can I watch TV?*—reminded her of him, and she would be at the fence again, feeling her heartbeat in her palm as he held her hand, as if her heart had never quite beat before he touched her. In her daydream, that moment ended differently. Not with him waving goodbye on his porch, but with him folding her into his arms, at last able to be together in the way they should have been all along.

"Sure. I'll take first bath. Remember, the front door stays shut and locked. You don't open it for anyone. And give Nana a call. Tell her we made it."

An hour later, they were both washed and cooled down, their wet hair dampening the backs of their nightgowns as they ate Pringles in bed, watching old cartoons. Georgia started to get sleepy, and snuggled into Holly's side, her legs curled up under her. She'd dropped her Pringle to pick up Kitty. Catty had a spot on the pillow on the other side of her.

Holly closed the can of chips and placed it on the nightstand, brushed off her hands and picked up the remote. When she snapped off the TV, the room was bathed in utter darkness. She helped Georgia crawl under the sheets, and then she joined her. They would both be asleep in minutes, she thought. And good thing, since they would be up and on the road again early in the morning.

Georgia's breathing evened out, and Holly thought she'd already drifted off, but then her voice stirred the darkness.

"Mommy?"

"Mmm-hmm?"

"Did Daddy do something wrong?"

Holly blinked in the dark. She hadn't been prepared for this question. But of course Georgia would ask. How could she not?

"What do you mean?"

"There was a lot of yelling. And I heard him say mean things to you. And he pulled your hair. Was he mad at you?"

"He was mad at me, yes," Holly said. "And he took you away from the carnival without telling me, so I was scared. And I was mad at him. Taking you away without asking was wrong."

"Oh. So do you hate him now?"

Holly had been taught from a young age that those who hate walked around in darkness, and that hatred always only hurt you and not the other person. She had never considered this in relation to Brody, though. Did she hate him? She would never think it possible to love him again, and in a romantic sense, she never would. But she was taught to love or at the very least to forgive.

"No, I don't hate him. I hope he gets help so he makes better choices in the future."

There was another long pause. "Where did he go?"

Holly always wanted to tell Georgia the truth but wondered if sometimes it was better to hide things. "He's fine," she said. "He just had to go away for a while. I'm sure he'll come around again." Now she hoped she was lying.

"Mommy?"

"Yes, honey?"

"Do I have to do the soup commercial?"

"Why?"

"I don't like it. I can't say the words, and the director is mean."

"Well…" Holly still hadn't signed anything. And she and Lynne never even discussed the soup commercial. The Icefall deal had been too big. The soup commercial was going to be a little bit of extra change, but nothing to get excited about. "I'm sure it won't be as bad as you think. You'll have rehearsals and get to know him, and I'm sure he won't be as mean as everyone says he is. And you'll get the words with more practice. You seem to like the song."

"Yeah. Okay."

But her voice sounded anything but okay. She slithered around until she was on her side, and Holly turned to match her pose. She reached out in the darkness and rubbed Georgia's back, just like she used to do when Georgia was a toddler and resisting a nap.

"Georgia?"

"Yeah?"

"Do you like acting?"

"It's okay," Georgia said. "Sometimes I just want to play, but the directors never let me. And they get mad when I mess up."

"They don't get *mad*, mad," Holly said.

"Sometimes they do."

Yeah, Holly thought. *They really do.*

There was no arguing that.

"I want to go home," Georgia said, her voice sleepy and lazy.

"Me, too, honey. Me, too."

The problem was, for the first time ever, Holly felt like she was leaving it.

SIXTEEN

"There's America's sweetheart!" Lynne stood with her arms outstretched as if to take Holly and Georgia into them, but she remained standing behind her desk. Like everything in Hollywood, it was a gesture that was all for show. "Have a seat, have a seat. You look exhausted. Both of you."

"We are," Holly agreed. "We didn't get in until late last night. I almost postponed our meeting so we could sleep."

They all sat, and Lynne put on her reading glasses to look over the bundle of papers on her desk in front of her. "Well, after you sign this sweet deal, you'll sleep like babies." She peered at Holly over her glasses. "Where did you say you were, again?"

"Garnett, Kansas."

"Kansas! That's right. Ugh, I'm sure you're glad to be back in civilization, huh?"

"Um…" Holly felt the need to defend her home state and realized that this was a need she felt any time she told someone in California that she came from the mid-dle of the country. They wrinkled their noses and gave her pitying looks and about four times out of five, they asked her about cows, as if everyone in the Midwest was a bovine expert. She always just laughed along, even though in her heart, she knew that she came from a great place, no matter what anyone else thought.

It was a place where Frisbees soared over fences and brought with them a lifelong love…

"Anyway!" Lynne had already moved on, in her requisite topic-flitting style, a hummingbird always chasing the sweet nectar of the next dollar. "So they didn't come up quite as high as I expected them to."

"What?" Holly leaned forward. "You said it was a done deal. You said the ink was dry."

Lynne put out a hand to stop Holly. "And it was. It was. But, you know, the economy is struggling, and people aren't able to pay box office prices anymore. That's the real culprit here. Inflation. The people. Can't afford a ten-dollar movie ticket, but no problem watching their twenty-dollar-a-month streaming service on their thousand-dollar phones. They complain that actors make too much money and teachers too little, and they don't even consider there are small actors making small amounts of money. Not everyone is Tom Cruise, I tell them, and they still just…"

"How small?"

"Not as small as you're thinking, I can tell you that much. Just comparatively small, I suppose."

"How small?"

"When you consider that she's five and only has a handful of lines…it's a very good deal."

"How small, Lynne?" Holly reached over and slid

the contract out from under the agent's hand. She pulled it across the desk, Lynne babbling the whole time about experience and unions and professionalism and anything she could think of to smooth over the fact that Holly had driven fifteen hundred miles for a deal that wasn't.

She couldn't look at it.

She knew if she saw the dollar amount, she would be tempted to take it, no matter what it was. She would convince herself that it was still a good enough deal, even if it wasn't what she'd been expecting. She would settle, because that was what she had been doing her entire adult life: settling.

She'd wanted Georgia to have a life different from hers. One that was more secure. She didn't want Georgia to have to scrape and save and work three jobs. But in order to do that, she was asking Georgia to work her entire life, from childhood. She had all of her adulthood ahead of her to work and worry and want to be at home playing.

And this wasn't home. Not anymore. Actually, it never had been. It had been the place she ran away to when Brody left her. After running away from home with Brody. Running, running, running. She was always running.

The image of Ryan, standing on his porch, waving, popped into her head unbidden once again.

She'd run away from him, too.

And why?

Fear. He was willing to put himself out there, to tell

her exactly how he felt. And it matched how she felt. And still, she ran away.

"We'll get more for the next one. They're thinking at least five of these, you know. I'll talk them up. She'll be so huge by then, they won't be able to say no."

Lynne's words bounced off Holly. Next time. It was always next time. But she realized that no matter how much they offered next time, it still wouldn't feel like enough. It wouldn't be enough. For either of them. Because what they both wanted wasn't money.

She laid her palm flat on the paper.

"It's a no."

Lynne stopped midsentence, and then let out a breathy laugh. She reached over and slid the contract back to her side of the desk. "I know it's not the news you wanted to hear, but I assure you that you'll still be happy."

"No, thank you."

"We'll go over it together."

Holly stood and was almost surprised when her legs held her up. She reached for Georgia. "Come on, Gee."

"I've alarmed you. I'm certain that if you just sit back down and have a look, you'll be much more pleased than you think you will."

"It's a *no*, Lynne. Georgia doesn't want this anymore. I don't want it. We're going home."

Lynne scoffed. "To… Kansas?"

It hadn't sunk all the way in when she said it, and it sort of surprised her. Home was Kansas. Home was where there were tomato plants and hay mazes and Frisbees.

Home was where Ryan waited for her at the fence, pulling weeds, smiling, waving.

"Yeah," she said, incredulous. "The deal I have waiting for me there is way more lucrative." She tightened her hand around Georgia's and led her toward the door.

Lynne sputtered and huffed behind her. "You need to understand, Holly, that Georgia's career will never recover if you walk away from this deal."

"Georgia is five—she doesn't have a career," Holly said over her shoulder.

"She will never get offered another deal if you walk out that door."

"That's okay, I'm walking away from all of the deals." Holly stopped and spun to face Lynne. "Especially the soup commercial. It sounds like dog food."

An unhappy life was surprisingly easy to dismantle. Holly was struck, time and again, at how impossible obstacles turned out to be no real obstacle at all.

When she turned in her badge and apron at the supermarket, her boss didn't rant and rave like she'd expected him to. Instead, he asked questions about Garnett, congratulated her and shook her hand.

Most people were decent, even when you were telling them something they didn't want to hear.

She broke her apartment lease with what little money she had in savings. It wouldn't matter. Cheryl was overjoyed to hear that they were returning and began sprucing up the house for three. She told Holly she could stay as long as she liked—or at least until she got a job in Garnett, built up a little savings and got on her feet.

Which meant Holly would be living next to Ryan again, a fact that sent her heart beating faster every time she thought about it.

Georgia would go to the same school Holly had gone to. She would be replaced as Icefall, and if people worked the way Holly knew them to work, everyone would be incensed at first that Icefall had been replaced, and within two movies, would forget that the first Icefall had ever existed.

Holly wanted it that way.

Georgia called her Nana every day, making plans for all the things they would do, places they would see, plants they would plant. She was over the moon about the move and more like a child than Holly had seen her in some time.

It was only a few weeks before everything had been packed and crammed into Holly's car. They hit the road, singing songs and telling silly jokes and eating tacos, both of them eager to start their new lives.

The drive back to Garnett felt nowhere near as long as the drive from Garnett had been.

It just felt easier to come home when it was actually home.

SEVENTEEN

Ryan's first thought was that his eyes were deceiving him. That maybe Cheryl had gotten a car similar to Holly's. Or maybe she had a friend who drove that car. Or maybe he was misremembering Holly's car.

But then he heard Georgia's laughter and looked out his back window to see her in the garden with her grandmother. His heart panged as he watched for Holly to join them. Desire and longing and heartbreak all at once.

Try as he might to get over her, he couldn't. He'd finally just come to accept that there was no getting over her, and he might as well stop trying.

His mind went to all the reasons she could possibly be back, and none of them were good.

He finally caught Cheryl in the driveway.

"Hey, is, um, everything all right? With Holly?" he asked.

"Absolutely. She lives here now. Moved all the way from California."

"Moved? Georgia's not doing a movie?"

Cheryl shook her head. "Holly decided not to do

that. Said it caused more trouble than it was worth. She's still a little shaken up from the carnival incident, as I'm sure anyone would be." She leaned closer to him. "But between you and me, I think there's something else that brought her home. Would you like to come in? Say hello?"

A surge of alarm went through Ryan, and he took a step back. "Oh. No. I'm sure… I'm sure I'll see her around."

"Okay, well, you know the offer always stands. Come on over for a glass of tea or something. Georgia has me baking just about every day." She held up the grocery bag she was clutching. "So chances are good you can score some fresh-baked cookies if you do."

He smiled. "Now, that's the most tempting offer I've gotten all day."

But he knew he never would. Holly had left no uncertainty between them. She was home. But that didn't mean she was home for him.

The doorframe looked great, but the door itself looked shabby, and Ryan found himself outside painting it. He had a feeling it would only lead to more painting. First the frame, then the door, then the house, the shutters, the cabinets, the bathrooms…

He had a hard time concentrating on much of anything, now that Holly was home. All he could think about was wanting to see her, to be near her. The best he could do was physical labor. If he kept his muscles moving, he could keep his brain silent.

Still, he felt the pull of her no matter how hard he tried to ignore it. No matter how many things he painted.

It was that pull that made him stop with his paintbrush in midair and turn around.

There she was, coming across the backyard toward the fence, winding her fingers through the hem of her shirt timidly. She smiled and gave a shy wave—a trait he still found so adorable it was almost painful. He gazed at her, wondering if it would ever be possible to have the thought, *This woman could not get more beautiful.* It seemed impossible. Every time he saw her, she was more beautiful than the last.

He set the paintbrush across the top of the can and wiped his hands on a rag, then let himself be pulled to her by whatever invisible force existed between them.

They met at the fence.

"Looks pretty good. I like the color." She bit her lip and stared off over his shoulder at the painting he'd been doing. But her gaze was farther away than that.

"Thanks. It's sort of a never-ending project. I fix one thing and find another that needs to be fixed. I don't know what I'll do with myself when I run out of things to paint." Part of him really did wonder what he would do when that happened. Painting kept his mind off the things he didn't want to think about. It was his respite.

"I'm sure my mom has plenty of painting she'd love to have done."

"I'll let you borrow my paintbrush."

Holly reached across the fence and playfully swatted

his arm. At least she was back to the present, laughing with him, which was how they'd always connected best.

"I hear Brody got a court date," he said.

She nodded. "I got a notice about it."

"You going to go?"

"I sent in a statement. They don't need me. And it would really be okay with me to never see him again as long as I live."

"Unfortunately, you know he'll get out at some point."

"I know. I'll tackle that problem when it happens."

Ryan kicked at the bottom of the fence lightly, awkward as a junior high student, trying to figure out how to ask what he'd been wondering. He decided to just go for it.

"So why are you here? I thought Georgia was going to be working."

"She was, but she's not anymore."

"Uh-oh, what happened? Did they back out on you?"

"No, I backed out on them," she said. "I changed my mind. Georgia didn't love the work, and I figure she has the whole rest of her life to make decisions about job satisfaction. Why make her start so young?"

"Good call. Not a lot of people would be able to look past the money."

"Well, that is hard to do. That money was her future, you know? About ten times a day, I wonder if I made the right choice. I'm kind of kicking myself."

"It's the right choice. You're a good mom, Holly. A great one, actually. I've seen firsthand how much you love that kid, so I can speak with authority."

"It's just…" She paused, ducked her head, pushed a lock of hair behind her ear. "I had another reason to nix the deal and come home. A selfish reason."

"What?"

She looked up, so that they were gazing directly into each other's eyes. "You."

The word rocked him back on his feet a little. "Me?"

She curled her fingers over the top of the fence, as if she, too, were rocked and needed to hang on to something in order to get this out. "I wanted to come back here for you. For us."

He used his forefinger to lightly trace the length of her forefinger. He wasn't sure what to say. He wanted her to keep talking. To get at what he hoped she was getting at.

"Ryan, when you told me that you loved me and I ran away, it was because I was afraid. I think I've always been afraid of how much I care about you."

His chest filled with elation. She was going to say what he hoped she would. Finally, they were on the same page and willing to admit it.

"Care…about me. Like…the same way my grandma cares about me?" He grinned and traced the back of her hand with his finger. "Or…?"

She rolled her eyes. "You want me to say it? Fine. I'll say it. I love you. I loved you back then, and I love you now. I haven't done a lot of things right in my life, but loving you feels like the one right thing I've done."

"So to be clear, you're not talking about my grandma…"

She stomped a foot playfully. "Ryan! Come on! I'm trying to be serious here."

He reached up and brushed her cheek, then let it rest there while he looked into her eyes, his heart practically bursting out of his chest. "Hey," he said, his voice serious. "I'm glad you came back."

"Yeah?"

He nodded. "Yeah. Gives me a chance to finally kiss you."

He leaned forward and brought his lips to hers, his other hand curled over the fence. It was a kiss they'd both longed for since they were teenagers. It was everything Ryan had envisioned it to be—sweet and warm and perfect. He felt as if he were falling backward through the years, given a chance at a do-over that most people didn't get. Given a chance at love.

He pulled back and let his hand fall away from her face, let it cover her hand. Now that they'd created this connection, he never wanted to let it go.

Huh, he thought. Sometimes prayers really do get answered.

"I love you, Holly."

"Why don't you come to this side of the fence, then?" she asked.

"I thought you'd never ask." Holly took a couple steps back as Ryan braced himself and then hopped over in one leap.

"We have a gate, you know," she said, walking toward the back porch.

"I know," he said, grabbing her hand to stop her short. "But then it would have taken me longer to get to you.

And I think we've waited long enough." He pulled her into an embrace that stripped away all the years of secrets and pain.

They were together now.

Best friends, in love.

Forever.

EPILOGUE

Holly repeatedly checked the door, biting her bottom lip, sitting forward on the edge of her seat. Her heart thumped. Her hands were sweaty. She hadn't been this nervous in a long time.

Her phone buzzed, and she snatched it up. His photo stared back at her.

She'd gotten a text.

I'm almost there.

She fired a text back.

I saved you a seat. But you need to hurry. Curtain goes up in three.

Policing wasn't always the most predictable job in the world, and ever since Ryan decided he was going to go for becoming a detective, she'd learned to live with long and variable hours. He was trying to work his way up the ladder so he'd have enough money to send their daughter to college.

The door burst open, and Georgia strode in, her white-blond hair artfully wild. Holly hadn't seen her since graduation, and she looked gorgeous—the kind of tan one could only get by working on a cruise ship and playing in the sun and sand of exotic locales. She'd found her acting dream not on film but on stage. She loved the feedback of a live audience.

She hadn't been Icefall in years, yet people still recognized her. But in this theater, she was recognized more for playing Dorothy in *The Wizard of Oz*, a role that she took all the way to the state championship in her freshman year.

"Hey! I'm here!" she whispered. Even her whispers sounded like little chirps of talent. Holly stood and wrapped herself around her daughter, a hug that was cut short by Cheryl nudging her way in.

"Aren't you a sight for sore eyes?" Cheryl said into Georgia's hair.

"How was Bali?" Holly asked when they finally let go.

"Gorgeous," Georgia said. "And we have an amazing set that we're calling our Island Set. It feels like I'm on a permanent vacation. And… I met a boy."

"Oh, tell me everything," Cheryl said, scooting back so Georgia could take the seat between her mother and grandmother.

Holly's phone buzzed again. She flipped it to check. Parking. At that same moment, someone flashed the houselights.

"She'll have to tell us everything later. The show's about to start," she whispered.

Georgia plucked the program off her mom's lap and opened it. She gasped. "She goes by Kat now?"

Holly giggled. "She started right after you left. She said it reminded her of you."

When Holly had discovered she was pregnant, she and Ryan decided to let Georgia help name the baby. She'd begged for Kitty, but they'd put their foot down. They eventually settled on Katherine, so Georgia could call her Kitty. Instead, she called her Kat.

And now, Kat, the spitting image of her sister in just about every way, was about to make her high school musical debut.

"So guess who tried to contact me again," Georgia said with an eye roll.

Holly sighed. "Not Brody."

"Trying to get bail money out of me."

"He's in prison again?"

"Yep. Something about violating a restraining order. Honestly, I just did what I always do. Ignore, ignore, ignore."

Holly had been disappointed when she found out that Brody was back on the streets. And she'd been a nervous wreck when the first thing he'd done after he got out was try to forge a relationship with Georgia.

But prison had made Brody even more reckless than before. Even more criminal. He'd been in and out on various charges since then. Twice, Ryan had made the arrests.

The houselights flashed again, and with one last glance toward the doors, Holly slid back in her seat.

Ryan had never missed a show yet; he wasn't about to start now.

The lights dimmed. Georgia turned and mouthed *I'm so excited*, shadows painting her face. Holly beamed. She was excited, too.

Ryan bustled in just as music began to swell out of the pit.

"Hey," he whispered, giving Holly a quick peck on the cheek before sinking into his own seat on the aisle. He leaned over Holly to catch Georgia's eye. "You made it!"

"Wouldn't miss it," she whispered back. "It's my sister's first show."

Ryan reached across and gave Georgia's hand a quick squeeze. Then he snaked an arm around Holly's shoulder and settled in close. The lights blacked out, the music took off and a spotlight hit the curtain, which parted slightly and then lurched, lurched, lurched until it was all the way open.

The spotlight hit a halo of white-blond hair.

The only thing wrong about my big brother, Charlie Brown…

Holly smiled and let herself relax in her seat. She'd made it a long time all alone. She was proud of that. She'd made some mistakes—hadn't everyone?—and she'd put herself on the line. She'd raised two beautiful daughters. She'd found the love of her life, and she took the risk of loving him, even when the love seemed so big, it terrified her.

She was brave.

She knew that about herself.
Garnett, Kansas, hadn't changed a bit.
But she had.
And she was glad of it.

* * * * *

Get 3 FREE REWARDS!

We'll send you 2 FREE Books plus a FREE Mystery Gift.

Both the **Love Inspired**® and **Love Inspired**® **Suspense** series feature compelling novels filled with inspirational romance, faith, forgiveness and hope.

YES! Please send me 2 FREE novels from the Love Inspired or Love Inspired Suspense series and my FREE gift (gift is worth about $10 retail). After receiving them, if I don't wish to receive any more books, I can return the shipping statement marked "cancel." If I don't cancel, I will receive 6 brand-new Love Inspired Larger-Print books or Love Inspired Suspense Larger-Print books every month and be billed just $6.49 each in the U.S. or $6.74 each in Canada. That is a savings of at least 16% off the cover price. It's quite a bargain! Shipping and handling is just 50¢ per book in the U.S. and $1.25 per book in Canada.* I understand that accepting the 2 free books and gift places me under no obligation to buy anything. I can always return a shipment and cancel at any time by calling the number below. The free books and gift are mine to keep no matter what I decide.

Choose one:
- ☐ **Love Inspired Larger-Print** (122/322 BPA GRPA)
- ☐ **Love Inspired Suspense Larger-Print** (107/307 BPA GRPA)
- ☐ **Or Try Both!** (122/322 & 107/307 BPA GRRP)

Name (please print)

Address   Apt. #

City   State/Province   Zip/Postal Code

Email: Please check this box ☐ if you would like to receive newsletters and promotional emails from Harlequin Enterprises ULC and its affiliates. You can unsubscribe anytime.

Mail to the Harlequin Reader Service:
IN U.S.A.: P.O. Box 1341, Buffalo, NY 14240-8531
IN CANADA: P.O. Box 603, Fort Erie, Ontario L2A 5X3

Want to try 2 free books from another series? Call 1-800-873-8635 or visit www.ReaderService.com.

*Terms and prices subject to change without notice. Prices do not include sales taxes, which will be charged (if applicable) based on your state or country of residence. Canadian residents will be charged applicable taxes. Offer not valid in Quebec. This offer is limited to one order per household. Books received may not be as shown. Not valid for current subscribers to the Love Inspired or Love Inspired Suspense series. All orders subject to approval. Credit or debit balances in a customer's account(s) may be offset by any outstanding balance owed by or to the customer. Please allow 4 to 6 weeks for delivery. Offer available while quantities last.

Your Privacy—Your information is being collected by Harlequin Enterprises ULC, operating as Harlequin Reader Service. For a complete summary of the information we collect, how we use this information and to whom it is disclosed, please visit our privacy notice located at corporate.harlequin.com/privacy-notice. From time to time we may also exchange your personal information with reputable third parties. If you wish to opt out of this sharing of your personal information, please visit readerservice.com/consumerschoice or call 1-800-873-8635. **Notice to California Residents**—Under California law, you have specific rights to control and access your data. For more information on these rights and how to exercise them, visit corporate.harlequin.com/california-privacy.

LIRLIS23

Get 3 FREE REWARDS!

We'll send you 2 FREE Books plus a FREE Mystery Gift.

FREE
Value Over
$20

Both the **Harlequin® Special Edition** and **Harlequin® Heartwarming™** series feature compelling novels filled with stories of love and strength where the bonds of friendship, family and community unite.

YES! Please send me 2 FREE novels from the Harlequin Special Edition or Harlequin Heartwarming series and my FREE Gift (gift is worth about $10 retail). After receiving them, if I don't wish to receive any more books, I can return the shipping statement marked "cancel." If I don't cancel, I will receive 6 brand-new Harlequin Special Edition books every month and be billed just $5.49 each in the U.S. or $6.24 each in Canada, a savings of at least 12% off the cover price, or 4 brand-new Harlequin Heartwarming Larger-Print books every month and be billed just $6.24 each in the U.S. or $6.74 each in Canada, a savings of at least 19% off the cover price. It's quite a bargain! Shipping and handling is just 50¢ per book in the U.S. and $1.25 per book in Canada.* I understand that accepting the 2 free books and gift places me under no obligation to buy anything. I can always return a shipment and cancel at any time by calling the number below. The free books and gift are mine to keep no matter what I decide.

Choose one: ☐ **Harlequin**   ☐ **Harlequin**   ☐ **Or Try Both!**
             Special Edition   **Heartwarming**   (235/335 & 161/361
             (235/335 BPA GRMK)   **Larger-Print**   BPA GRPZ)
                                           (161/361 BPA GRMK)

Name (please print)

Address   Apt. #

City   State/Province   Zip/Postal Code

Email: Please check this box ☐ if you would like to receive newsletters and promotional emails from Harlequin Enterprises ULC and its affiliates. You can unsubscribe anytime.

Mail to the **Harlequin Reader Service:**
IN U.S.A.: P.O. Box 1341, Buffalo, NY 14240-8531
IN CANADA: P.O. Box 603, Fort Erie, Ontario L2A 5X3

Want to try 2 free books from another series! Call 1-800-873-8635 or visit www.ReaderService.com.

*Terms and prices subject to change without notice. Prices do not include sales taxes, which will be charged (if applicable) based on your state or country of residence. Canadian residents will be charged applicable taxes. Offer not valid in Quebec. This offer is limited to one order per household. Books received may not be as shown. Not valid for current subscribers to the Harlequin Special Edition or Harlequin Heartwarming series. All orders subject to approval. Credit or debit balances in a customer's account(s) may be offset by any outstanding balance owed by or to the customer. Please allow 4 to 6 weeks for delivery. Offer available while quantities last.

Your Privacy—Your information is being collected by Harlequin Enterprises ULC, operating as Harlequin Reader Service. For a complete summary of the information we collect, how we use this information and to whom it is disclosed, please visit our privacy notice located at corporate.harlequin.com/privacy-notice. From time to time we may also exchange your personal information with reputable third parties. If you wish to opt out of this sharing of your personal information, please visit readerservice.com/consumerchoice or call 1-800-873-8635. **Notice to California Residents**—Under California law, you have specific rights to control and access your data. For more information on these rights and how to exercise them, visit corporate.harlequin.com/california-privacy.

HSEHW23

HARLEQUIN
PLUS

Try the best multimedia subscription service for romance readers like you!

Read, Watch and Play.

Experience the easiest way to get the romance content you crave.

Start your **FREE TRIAL** at
<u>www.harlequinplus.com/freetrial</u>.